GW01402898

THE GUILTY SUITCASE

By

Eileen Dickson
Elaine Douglas
Vera Morris
Julie Roberts
Eve Wibberley

Jeeve Publishing

First published in Great Britain in 2007 by
Jeeve Publishing
PO Box 2696
Reading RG1 9BQ
Email: jeevepublishing@aol.com
and info@jeevestories.co.uk
Website: www.jeevestories.co.uk

Copyright © 2007 Text Eileen Dickson, Elaine Douglas,
Vera Morris, Julie Roberts, Eve Wibberley

Copyright © 2007 Cover and Illustrations Sue Tait

All rights reserved. No part of this publication may be
reproduced, stored in a retrieval system, or transmitted, in any
form or by any means, electronic, mechanical, photocopying,
recording or otherwise, without prior permission, in writing,
from the copyright holders.

The authors assert their moral right to be identified as
authors of this work

The stories are works of fiction. Any resemblance to actual
persons, living or dead, events or locations are entirely
coincidental.

ISBN 978-0-9550522-1-7

Printed and bound in Great Britain by
Ridgeway Press, Ltd. Bramley, Hampshire

We wish to thank everyone who helped and supported us.

Our chosen charity
Thames Valley and Chiltern Air Ambulance Trust

Contents

FISHY LADIES AT *LA CAVERNA*

'My fishy ladies! Welcome to *La Caverna*!' cried Salvatore as he saw the five women, Julie, Elaine, Eileen, Vera and Eve standing in the doorway of his Italian restaurant.

Fishy ladies? they thought. Last year it was 'The Swanwick Babes'.

'So, you have come for your annual visit to Derbyshire?'

'We have,' said Julie, 'and our week always starts with a visit to Matlock Baths and lunch at *La Caverna.*'

Salvatore, resplendent in white chef's jacket, blue and white striped apron with a tea-towel tucked in the waist-band, beamed at them. 'Lady Writers! Please – which table would you like?' He gestured around the room. The walls were white stucco and there was white china on the checked tablecloths.

'I love this place,' said Elaine, 'it's *so* Italian!'

Salvatore smiled at them indulgently. He was slim, maturely handsome, a silvered moustache beneath a Roman nose.

They decided on a table in the inner room so that they could watch Salvatore preparing their meals in the small open kitchen behind a counter on which stood a tall glass vase containing flowers; strings of garlic dangled on the side walls.

Every year the five women, all addicted to writing, came to the *Writers' Summer School* at Swanwick. On their first visit, searching for a place to eat they had wandered down the main street looking for somewhere special. A sign, promising Italian food, led them down a narrow passageway carved from the limestone cliffs that towered over the town. At the end of the passage was *La Caverna*: a romantic courtyard, and two rooms.

1

The Guilty Suitcase

In the inner room, behind a glass screen, was a grotto filled with running water and plants. An exotic water-hole in the Derbyshire Dales.

Delicious aromas drifted from the kitchen as Salvatore cooked their chosen dishes with his usual skill and panache. The five women raised their glasses of wine.

'To another successful week at Swanwick!' said Eve.

'Next year we'll be bringing our second book with us,' said Eileen. 'We *must* decide on a theme soon.'

They all nodded, worried expressions temporarily replacing celebratory smiles.

Later, after an excellent meal, Salvatore brought coffee and amoretti. 'Ladies, I did enjoy your book, *Fish Pie and Laughter*, which is why I always think of you as my Fishy Ladies.' He bowed and retreated to his kitchen.

'I love Italian men,' said Vera, *sotto voce*, 'they are so simpatico! So open, so expressive – not afraid to show their emotions.'

There was silence. Five sets of grey-matter simultaneously whirred.

'Emotions!' they collectively exclaimed. And so the theme for this book was found.

'Salvatore, you're an inspiration!' cried Vera.

Looking puzzled, Salvatore modestly bowed again and continued grating the Parmesan cheese.

Vera

THE BRIDE WORE BROWN

The Fishy Ladies had chosen as their permanent watering hole The Unicorn, a pub in the Oxfordshire countryside. It served excellent food and the two friendly landlords, who didn't mind them occupying a table for three hours on Saturday lunchtime, while they read their stories and made a lot of noise.

'Look!' Vera pointed at the marquee on the lawn of The Unicorn, 'It must be a wedding.' The spring sunshine gilded the tent and smoothed a golden patina over the figures on the lawn of the inn. The five women admired the bride, fancied the groom and moved indoors to order drinks.

'I'm glad I didn't have a white wedding!' said Vera.

Julie, Eve, Eileen and Elaine looked at her aghast. 'You didn't have a proper wedding!'

'I certainly didn't! I refused to invite any relatives and friends. We had two witnesses and my mother - who insisted on attending. I wore a brown suit, which I'd made myself – I looked rather natty – Vogue pattern of course. Later we had a party and when the guests arrived they gave us brown paper envelopes containing money.'

'I didn't know you had Mafia connections,' said Eve.

*Vera looked at their pitying faces. 'Don't feel sorry for me. We were madly in love and it **was** different!'*

Their faces relaxed – in love – well, that's all right then.

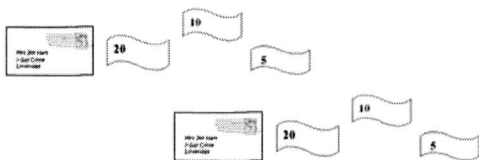

3

Love in a Eggcup

Ingrid pushed open the door of the department store and stepped into the cold January air. Her quick movement, as she tossed the scarf over her shoulder, betrayed her frustration. I'll never find a suitable present for him at this rate, she thought.

She walked away from the main shopping centre of the town to the older part, with its narrow streets and smaller shops. The windows reflected her image – a tall, elegant woman, with handsome features – but she was unaware of the admiring glances of passers-by as she searched for inspiration.

After abortive sorties into a book shop, men's outfitters and a leather shop, she stopped in front of a display of antiques. In the centre of the window was a mantel clock: it had a clear dial, stylish mahogany case and four round brass feet. He would love it! She twisted her head to try to read the price tag, but it was obscured by a pair of silver serving spoons.

Ingrid hesitated; antique shops and their owners made her feel insecure. The antiques were usually close together and narrow aisles and breakable china added to her uncertainty. The owners were often pushy and she knew she would be expected to bargain; if she accepted the price as stated she would be paying over the odds.

She tried to push away the feelings of vulnerability and panic that sometimes returned to her. Get a grip of yourself, she thought, you're thirty nine, loved by your husband and family and you run a successful business. Get in there!

*

'Good morning. Anything special you're looking for?'

'I'd like to look round if that's all right?' Wouldn't do to head for the clock straight away, she thought.

The woman at the desk smiled and continued writing price tags. Ingrid decided to tour the shop before casually asking about the clock. The shop stretched out like the Tardis: first, small pieces of furniture; then china and silver in cabinets; lastly small items crowded together on shelves. There were Doulton figurines, Goss memorabilia ... a row of eggcups!

Ingrid remembered eggcups on the windowsill of her childhood home and the flowers she and Paul had picked in the woods. She remembered their closeness and friendship. Her fingers brushed over the display: Humpty Dumpty, a rabbit, a chicken. Her hand stopped - there it was. Her special eggcup. It was a simple shape covered in an iridescent glaze of different colours: pink, green, blue, silver. She lifted it from the shelf and clasped it in her hand . . .

'Mummy, can I bring a friend to tea after school?'

'Who is it? Do we know the family?'

'His name's Paul; he lives round the corner. He said he lives in a flat. What's a flat? I didn't like to ask him.'

My mother turned to my father, 'You *know* who they are, don't you? That isn't his real father - she's divorced.' She turned back to me, 'Why did you make friends with this boy? Why can't you bring a nice girl home for tea?'

'Let the child make friends where she can; she hasn't made many since we moved here.' My father rose from the breakfast table, picking up his paper.

'What can you expect; bringing us to a town that's half deserted. I suppose it was the only way you could get promotion in the bank; to take a job no one else wanted.'

The Guilty Suitcase

I decided to leave for school.

Our house was near the sea front – you couldn't go on the beach because they hadn't cleared away the mines, but you could see the sea through the barbed wire. The town wasn't really deserted, but lots of houses had been damaged by bombs. I'd played in some of them with Paul – I told my mother I was going to the rec to play on the swings and roundabout. The gardens of the houses were overgrown, with tiger lilies and lupins poking from between the weeds. We would climb the iron fire-escapes and scramble in through broken windows. The floor boards would creak and we would scream with fear and delight as we imagined the house collapsing in a mass of bricks and plaster dust.

'Mummy, can I go to Paul's after tea? His mum wants to meet me.'

She turned away from the potatoes and looked at me suspiciously. 'Have you tidied your bedroom?'

'Yes,' I lied.

'And polished your shoes for tomorrow?'

'No, but I'll do them before I go.'

'Very well, but you must wear your second-best frock. You can't go in that one, it looks grubby. Why you can't keep a dress clean for a week, I don't know. That comes from playing with boys.' She returned to the potatoes, attacking the eyes with vicious twists of the peeler.

I decided to go upstairs and sort out my bedroom.

Daddy had told me about flats and I was happy as I skipped up the steps to Paul's front door. He opened it, grinned at me, grabbed my hand and pulled me in.

'Mum! Here's Ingrid,' he shouted.

The sitting room had a cream carpet, there were flowers in a jug on the table and a gas fire was hissing blue flames. The velvet curtains were drawn against the January gloom. A woman with dark hair, glinting with red, a book on her lap, was sitting on a sofa. I had seen her before, but only at a distance. She was lovely, she had a bright red mouth and long red fingernails. She put down the book, got up, and took my hand.

'Hello, Ingrid. Paul has told me how much fun you have together. Would you like some hot chocolate?'

I nodded, dumbstruck. 'Gosh, she's ever so pretty, Paul,' I whispered as she went into the kitchen.

'She's the best Mum in all the world,' he said proudly.

I agreed with him. Paul didn't look like her; he had brown, curly hair and bright blue eyes. I wondered if he looked like his father.

Later, after the hot chocolate and *two* biscuits, she started talking about Paul's eighth birthday party. And I was invited!

Then I realised the date. 'But that's my birthday too!'

Paul and I looked at each other and grinned. We had the same birthday.

'Are *you* having a party? What a pity. You won't be able to go to each other's,' she said

'No, I'm not having a party this year; I can come to Paul's.' I had instantly decided that Paul's parties would be much more fun than mine. My mother's idea of a children's party was to have lots of competitions, including spelling-bees, which I usually won. The guests, never more than five well-behaved girls, soon became disenchanted.

In the winter we played on the wooded cliff near our homes. It was exciting exploring the narrow, steep paths and sliding in the mud. We found a wooden box and tobogganed down; the bushes whizzed by and stones shot out sideways. There were flowers in the wood: snowdrops and later, primroses. Once I took Paul to my house and we arranged the flowers in the egg cups which I kept on a windowsill. I had seven egg cups: a cockerel, with gay, painted feathers, Mickey Mouse, whose big ears stuck out around the breakfast egg; he looked as though he had an enormous bump - perhaps Minnie had hit him with a frying pan. My favourite egg cup was a beautiful oval, with a slender stem and magic rainbow colours. It was the most beautiful thing in the world.

I explained all this to Paul, who listened intently as he helped me to fill the eggcups with the flowers.

'Aren't they lovely, Mummy?'

She came over from the ironing board, 'You've both done them very nicely,' she said, blowing her nose. 'Would you like a cup of cocoa?'

One morning in school the headmistress addressed our class. 'We have received your eleven-plus results. I will read out the names of the pupils who will be going to the Grammar School in September.'

I looked at Paul and we smiled. We usually came near the top of the class. We talked about what it would be like; we would learn French and go on the French exchange.

The headmistress read out the names. She didn't call our names out. We turned to each other. I could see astonishment in Paul's eyes and I felt sick.

'Our Head boy and Head girl this year are Paul and Ingrid. They have passed with flying colours and have won scholarships to public schools.'

We walked home together. 'What will your mother say when you tell her?' said Paul.

'That I've passed with flying colours? I don't know. I don't want to go to that boarding school. What will you do?'
  'I shall go. I'd like to get away.'
  'I thought you loved your Mum?'
  'I do, but I don't like *him.*'
  'What are flying colours, Paul?'

I went to the grammar school. That year everything changed. My father wasn't at home. Mummy said he had to go away because of work. When I went to play with other children, their parents would come to the door and tell me to go away; no one could come out to play. Paul was at boarding school.

One day, on the way home from school, a girl came up to me. 'Your dad's a gaolbird; he stole money from the bank!' She pulled my hair and ran away. Now I knew why Mummy cried at night when she thought I was asleep. I didn't tell her about the girl.

My father came back, thin and grey. We were to move to the Midlands to live with my Grandmother. My toys would go in an auction; there wasn't room for them in Gran's house. The doll's house, the pram, the two Christmas trees and their decorations - all to be sold. I watched sadly as they were put in boxes or lot numbers were tied to them. In the madness of moving, the egg cups disappeared. I couldn't even say goodbye to Paul.

Ingrid waited impatiently for her husband to come back from taking the dogs for a walk. She'd hidden the clock in her wardrobe, but the egg cup, crammed with snowdrops, was on the window sill. She heard the back door open, the dogs' claws skittering on the conservatory floor and a jangle as leads were hung up on the wall.
  'We're back! Kettle on?'

He came in, his bright blue eyes smiling, his hair, though touched with grey, curling tightly from the winter mist.

'Why are you sitting in the gloom? Are you all right?' he asked anxiously.

Ingrid pointed to the windowsill, 'Look, Paul! Our egg cup!'

He laughed and took her hand and raised it to his lips. For a moment they were children again.

Vera

Of Love and Chickens

Every morning the young woman watched from her cottage window, as the Italian prisoners of war were driven down the lane in the lorry to the farm where they were working.

They were so young, she thought - some no more than boys, probably didn't know what they were doing in the cold Sussex countryside, hauling vegetables from frozen earth.

'Don't you go wasting sympathy on them,' sniffed Minnie Bowman who kept the village shop. 'Got it easy they have, nothing to what Our Boys are going through.'

'But at least it's sunny in Benghazi,' countered Ellen, who didn't like Ma Bowman - Minnie had favourites and kept things under the counter for them. Ellen was not one of these.

Walking home from the village through cold spring air, Ellen idly wondered about the Italians crowded into the tiny cottage that had been the gamekeeper's before the war. There was only a well, she knew, and an Elsan toilet in a shed at the bottom of the garden. Across the darkening fields a dog fox barked harshly for its mate. Long time since she'd had a mate, Ellen thought ruefully, and hurried home to her cottage and a warming pot of tea, although only sweepings were left in the caddy by this time in the month.

'It'll all be over by Christmas, love, you'll see - Winnie'll wop those Hun's backsides, see if he don't.' Bill, her husband of fourteen months, had exulted, returning with his mates from the Recruiting Office in East Grinstead. He smelt of beer, and staggered slightly.

'You're looking forward to this, aren't you?' said Ellen accusingly. 'What about me, and the hens and everything

11

here?' she'd demanded. She'd always been afraid of the vicious cockerel with the wall eye.

'If I can fight the Germans, then you can deal with a few bloody old hens,' he'd countered, suddenly angry. He knew she was right, guilty now the beer and bravado had worn off.

Ellen noticed that a tall young man with a limp sometimes walked back by himself after the lorry had returned in the evening. He wore a red bandanna at his neck. He would smile politely and raise a hand in greeting. One evening, she'd been in the front garden trying to catch silly Rosie the Leghorn who was always escaping. She'd given them all names by this time and found herself talking to them; it was company.

'You want I should help?' he asked her.

Flustered, she had replied, 'No, well, yes,' when with a quick grab he had retrieved the flighty chicken which was now tucked quietly into his chest.

'Thank you, you are very good with chickens,' she blurted out.

'Is easy, we have at home,' he replied. 'I will put back in their house?'

'In England, it's a *coop*,' she enunciated very carefully.

'Ah, I understand, like being *cooped up*?' he replied. 'Like as we are?'

Ellen was thrown off balance by his good English and didn't know how to reply, 'S'pose so.'

He smiled and deftly returned the now almost comatose chicken to her.

Ellen felt absurdly jealous of the chicken.

That night she lay in bed, listening to the owls hooting in Top Wood, and touched herself in the places that she had tried not to. Hot, swift, moist gratification came to her, but she felt cheated. Why had Bill gone off before he need, leaving her like this? She turned over to a cool bit of their double bed and thought of the Italian at the end of the lane. His brown arms had been smooth, but his hands would be hard and calloused. Was this treachery? Betrayal of trust? But she'd done nothing wrong. She slept badly that night.

Ellen found herself doing small gardening jobs in the front garden around six o'clock. She had dabbed on some precious Coty facepowder and a little lipstick, telling herself that it was important to keep up appearances. He walked past three evenings later; the days were growing longer and the blackbird was opening his throat from the blossoming apple tree.

'How are hens?' he asked her, smiling.

'Hens are fine, but I'll need to make their house safer against Reynard.'

'Reynard?' he queried, black brows raised in an arc of enquiry, 'and is *coop*, I think.'

'Naughty old dog box, he eats chickens,' she said, laughing.

'Then we have to keep out. You have nails and wood?'

It was only manners, she thought, to invite him to supper. 'Killed a pig down Women's Institute this week,' Ellen said. 'Would you like to join me - as a thank you, like?'

'Fierce English Women then,' he'd said. 'Thank you.'

Ellen unearthed a bottle of Elderberry wine. She sparkled, unused to the alcohol. She had not cooked for a man in some while. At some point, she must have reached out and touched his hand, seeking his gaze.

He stood up suddenly, the wooden chair scraping harshly against the tiled floor. 'I have wife; I cannot come again. Thanks for kindness.'

Nothing had happened, but something had been broken.

She watched him limping down the lane in the fading light, and felt anger and - shame.

13

A week later the prisoners were moved on. The local children raced through the village street after the lorry shouting *Italiana, Sultana,* but the Italians just grinned and waved back. Later, she found a carved wooden toy of pecking chickens on her doorstep. The scrawled message said, *For your child, when all are come safely home, Sergio.*

He had gone, but she was the prisoner. Ellen slammed it into a drawer and went to shut up the hens.

The toddler was sitting on the rag mat playing with a wooden toy. As the weight dropped, a chicken popped up and he shrieked in delight.

'Where'd you get that funny old thing?' Bill asked idly, stretched out in the armchair. He was still in his milking overalls and smelt faintly of cow.

Ellen replied 'Don't rightly remember,' and smiled.

Eileen

Churned with Love

Churned with Love is the caption for a butter advertisement but it's a good description of what happens to men and women when they fall in love. Mixed-up and agitated. Look at Lucy sitting in front of her computer, hands poised over the keyboard, grinning inanely, and gazing starry-eyed at the screen. From here I can't see what programme she's using but at a guess it's not *Excel*. Whoops, here comes trouble. No, she's quick enough to bang a few keys as the boss walks by. Her face is scarlet and she knows it.

Time to go home to my dogs and I meet her in the cloakroom where she's carefully adjusting her make-up and brushing her long fair hair.

'Where are you off to then?'

'Never you mind,' she replies as she flounces off.

She's right. It's none of my business. I'm old enough to be her mother and she's unlikely to confide in me. In my head I can see my tall, elegant mother saying, 'Have you told me everything? It'll all end in tears.' I hate to admit it but she was right. She would know wouldn't she? She managed to get through several lovers in her lifetime. I almost gave up counting after I left home. 'Tis better to have loved and lost than never to have loved at all,' she'd titter but I do feel she overdid it. Was it worth the bitter recriminations and traumas at the end of each relationship or the despondency and misery during the lull before the start of a new one?

The first love in her life that I knew about was Arthur, my father. Tall and good-looking, every woman's dream, it seems. Apart from the ladies he had another love - whisky. He was a salesman and whenever possible mother sent me out with him presuming he wouldn't go to the pub with a small child in tow. Crisps and pop were sent out to me in the car. He died young but not before he'd landed a few black eyes on mother whilst in his cups. She sent him packing. Some people muttered that she was enough to 'drive anyone to drink.' Perhaps there was some truth in that. She loved shopping and was forever demanding money. My aunts had never seen anyone with so many pairs of shoes. I thought it was normal and confess to a passion for footwear myself. She and Imelda Marcos had much in common.

Harry, an American soldier in his well-tailored uniform, with silk stockings to woo the girls and sweets for the kids, was next on the list. I described him as 'tall with a drawl,' which annoyed mother. He didn't live with us, but visited frequently. He'd come roaring up to the house in his jeep, leap out over the side into my mother's open arms. With a fistful of chewing gum, I was sent out to play and told not to come back till bedtime. I heard my friend's mother, arms akimbo, head nodding knowingly in my direction, tutting to her neighbour over the fence, 'They're overpaid, oversexed and over here.' Something like that had been said on the wireless but I couldn't think what it had to do with me. Harry disappeared after a few months and we never heard from him again, so I lost my extra sweet supply to barter with at school and mother was miserable once more.

Not for long. Harry seemed to have given her a taste for men in uniform but I was startled when the police car pulled up outside our house. Mike must have started life somewhere in Ireland from his accent but I have no idea where mother met him. With a wink, he told me she was going *to help him with his enquiries.* Sometime later, Mike moved in but as he worked shifts I didn't see him very much, thank goodness. I was now in my teens and if mother happened to be out when he came home, it was very obvious that he wanted me *to help him with his enquiries*. I soon learnt to nip out of the back door when I heard his key in the lock. Whilst I was away at secretarial college, Mike was implicated in a scandal and he had left by the time I came home for the summer vacation. Years later I discovered that he, with several of his colleagues and some ladies-of-the-night were accused of using the prison cells at the police station for activities other than the retention of criminals. It was all hushed up but Mike left the police force and presumably, without his uniform, he lost mother as well.

When I started work, I lived in a hostel and went home occasionally at weekends. One Friday evening I got the shock of my life. My cousin's husband, Tom, had seemingly left his wife and taken up residence with us. Only temporarily, I was assured, till he could sort things out at home. He was an air-force officer and another man who couldn't keep his hands to himself. In time the 'temporary' became 'permanent' and my cousin divorced him. Mother and Tom eventually married till death did them part.

Going through her papers after the funeral, I came across my parents' marriage certificate which was dated two years after I was born. I was also surprised to learn that she'd been married previously. So there was another love I never knew.

What a life. Is it any wonder I decided never to declare, 'I do,' to anyone and bought a dog instead? Mind you, I've had moments of weakness but my beloved dogs have always seen them off.

Eve

Love Story

I emerge into the reception area at Heathrow and look for a placard with my name on it. Ah yes, there it is, *Mrs Nesbett Brown* clearly printed, held up by a thickset man of around forty, wearing a denim jacket and jeans. We acknowledge each other and he introduces himself as Trevor's cousin. He asks me to follow him to the car park and takes my pull-along Louis Vuitton case. We stop in front of a Morgan and after depositing the case in the small boot, I too am safely deposited in the car. He jumps into the driving seat turns on the ignition and off we go. Thank goodness I have a large silk scarf to cover my hair.

We drive for a little over an hour through the leafy lanes of Oxfordshire, so different from the open Veldt of my homeland, to Watlington, the smallest town in England, and pull up outside a rambling old cottage setback from the lane. As we walk up the path the front door opens and a simply dressed and quietly confident English lady welcomes us inside.

'Do come in Annette. I may call you by your first name, I hope? I'm Sarah. I'm sorry your husband couldn't be with you. Everyone else is down at the church for a rehearsal but they'll be back soon. Let's have a cup of tea and get to know one another before everyone descends on us.'

An hour later everyone does indeed descend on us, filling the sitting room with laughter and chatter. The first to greet me is my daughter, Marianne.

'Hello, Mummy darling. I am so happy to see you. Did you have a good journey? Let me introduce you to everyone. David, this is my mother. Mummy, this is my fiancé, Trevor, the wonderful man whose wife I will become to-morrow and this is ...'

'David!' I say. We look at each other.

'Annette! Is it possible? Is it really you?'

In front of me stands a tall, slightly stooping figure, his face, although tired, has strong features and soft kind brown eyes and, yes, those healing hands now clasping mine.

The years fall away and I remember the upright strong young doctor, full of energy and hope, with a mission to heal the sick, poverty-stricken and forgotten people of Africa. Who did David see in front of him? An elegant, sophisticated and rather selfish woman of a certain age or did he remember the young adventurous, independent and fun-loving creature who had adored him and teased him for being too serious about life?

'Yes, it is and how coincidental that our offspring will marry tomorrow,' I gasp.

'How do you know each other?' exclaims Marianne.

'We met a long time ago in Cape Town,' answers David, 'our paths crossed but I would never have guessed Marianne was your daughter, Annette.'

'Marianne is very like her father was,' I reply.

'Mum!' calls Trevor, 'Annette and Dad met years ago in Cape Town. Isn't that amazing?'

The church is packed to bursting, the scent of the flowers all around reminding me of another wedding, twenty-five years ago in a similar setting in the Cape, when I married Marianne's father. Such a happy day, full of promise but tragedy was to strike a few months later when my husband went into the burning house of a neighbour and brought out a toddler under his jacket. But as he stumbled out onto the stoop, a piece of burning timber struck him and he died of his injuries on the way to hospital. The child, thankfully, survived, but Marianne was born without ever seeing her father.

The Guilty Suitcase

*

The happy couple walk down the aisle and out into the sunshine. Then photographs and later we go to the local hotel a few hundred yards away for the reception. The guests are enjoying the delicious smoked salmon and champagne and the lovely surroundings, so very English. The groom is now extolling the virtues of his wife: loving, caring, interested in people, a gentle girl, but with a will and determination of her own and hidden strength.

Perhaps she derives the strength from her stepfather's influence. Jack, a pilot, insisted that Marianne needed a father and I, a loving husband. We were happy together and I was ambitious to see the world outside Africa. Jack worked for a company in Libya, flying back and forth to the oilrigs with supplies and people. I found this new life in a different culture fascinating and soon made friends and really took to the expatriate life. Its small community reminded me of Cape Town. Sadly, this ended again in tragedy when, on a routine return flight from an oilrig, the engine failed and the helicopter went up in flames with my darling, courageous Jack trapped inside. If only our little son had not been stillborn the year before. I felt utterly bereft and returned to the loving cradle of my family in South Africa once more.

What a charming scene on this sunny happy day here in England. Marianne is lucky to have married into such a warm loving family and Sarah will understand and nurture her when the babies come, as they surely will.

'Thank you, David, I'd love to dance. Well, this takes me back a long time when we used to dance all night together.'

'Annette, you certainly look fantastic. Life must have treated you well.'

'Looks can be deceiving, David, but I think that you have had a happy and fulfilling life with Sarah. Our children are a perfect match and this has been a wonderful day for me. Before I journey home tomorrow perhaps I could talk with Sarah and yourself privately, but now I think I will have to sit down. Age catching up, I'm afraid.'

'Are you all right, Annette? You seem to be overly tired.'

'If I could have a glass of water, David. I'll just sit down and catch my breath for a while.' If only I didn't feel so tired.

It took about six months after Jack died for me to make sense of my life. My sister suggested that Marianne and I went to stay with her in Rome. Her family lived in a sprawling old villa and a complete change of lifestyle could only be for the best. She was, of course, correct and once settled with my daughter in Rome, I began to take an interest in my new surroundings. Marianne, like most young children, adapted quickly to her new life, loved school and seemed happy being part of a large family with her cousins. I began socialising at last, being drawn into dinner parties and met an interesting group of people. It wasn't long before I was introduced to Robert Nesbett Brown. Everywhere I went he was there, attentive, charming and so helpful, planning visits to Florence, Siena and the surrounding places near Rome.

Over the next few months, Robert and I became good friends and then lovers. A widower near retiring age, he was posted as British Ambassador to Berne and so we married and went to Switzerland. It all seems such a long time ago.

'Mummy, are you very tired? Such a long day for you. Trevor and I are leaving soon. We'll come and visit you in Switzerland, I promise. Just think, if we hadn't gone to live

21

there, I wouldn't have met Trevor. Sarah is going to take you back to the house now. Goodnight, darling Mummy.'

Here I am on the flight back to Berne. Such a rush to get to Heathrow, no time to talk to Sarah and David. I shall have to write to them in a few days. Robert will be at the airport to meet me and we will drive up into the mountains where we have our holiday chalet; there I can rest and attend the nearby clinic where I will get the very best medical care.

My journey through life has been full and varied. Blessed with good fortune, mixed with great sadness. I have experienced great heights and great depths of emotion but above all I have received love in vast quantities and have given in return. Love is all encompassing, love is everything.

Elaine

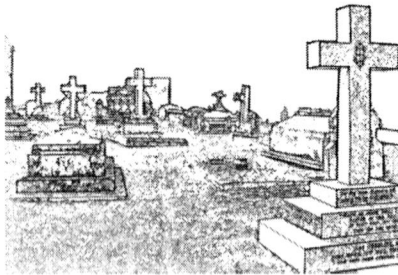

Jorja's Resolution

'I have your diary,' said a male voice.

Jorja Philips held the mobile phone at arm's length and counted to ten, then flipped her straight dark hair back over her shoulder and brought the phone back to her ear. This was a new tack to chat up a girl, 'Who am I speaking to and I have not lost my diary.'

'Karl Bennett, and I assure you I do have it.'

Jorja felt her heartbeat quicken. There was so much personal rubbish scribbled in those pages. 'Hold on a second please.' Putting the phone down, she snatched her handbag from the desk drawer. It weighed a ton. Why did she carry so much? She rummaged round make-up, letters, supermarket receipts and *two* wallets – why two? Half the cards were out of date and useless. Frustrated, she emptied the contents onto the desktop. It wasn't there. She pulled the lining out willing it to appear like magic.

'So … you have my diary. Where did you find it?'

'In the park. Under the seat, by the rose garden.'

He was so controlled, authoritative and now that the initial panic had eased, she liked the sound of his voice.

'Where did you get my number?'

'From your diary. Where else would I get it?'

'You've been reading my diary! How dare you pry into my …'

'Hey, I only looked at the detail page. How else was I going to know who to call?' His manner changed. 'I'm not a peeping Tom, if that's what you think.'

'Sorry, it's just …' Jorja felt so stupid and her cheeks burnt with humiliation. 'Can you post it back to me, please. You have the address.'

'I've a better idea. Have lunch with me. 12.30 in the park.'

He didn't wait for an answer, and it left her no choice if she wanted the diary back.

Jorja sat on the edge of the park seat, head down, feeling more like a honeybee than the stinging wasp on the phone earlier. A pair of long legs filled her view and a voice asked, 'Hello. Are you Jorja Philips?'

She looked up, 'Yes. You're Karl Bennett?' Of course he was. What a dumb thing to say and she bit her lower lip to stop it trembling. Big girls don't cry, but she was so nervous. Was this how a blind date started? Two strangers, eyeing each other up and wondering what they had let themselves in for? What if he was a serial killer, a rapist or a kidnapper? He didn't look evil. In fact, she liked what she saw. Stop, she warned herself, keep it strictly business. Get the diary and go. He sat down beside her. She caught the tang of aftershave on his rugged face and his complexion hinted moors and mountains. Even sitting down she had to tilt her head to look into his green eyes and his hair was the colour of a new thatch.

Jorja smiled and two dimples dented her cheeks.

He raised an eyebrow, 'Am I such a clown?'

'No, of course not. I'm sorry, I didn't mean to be rude.'

'No offence taken. Are you ready for lunch?' He took a brown takeaway bag from behind his back.

Jorja blinked in surprise. This was lunch? Sandwiches at a park bench. What had she expected, a three course *á la carte* at the Ritz? Seated, served, eaten and back to the office within an hour. Wake up girl! This is reality, a hurried snack out of a bag.

'This is kind of you.'

'My pleasure, Jorja. I hope you like chicken and mayonnaise. It's what my sister eats, so I assumed …'

'Yes, I do.' As she took the cellophane pack from him her fingers brushed his. They were warm, slightly hardened. Yet he wore a dark business suit.

They sat in the shade of a tree, relaxed, no awkwardness between them. He told her he was an architect - not yet famous - but there was time. She guessed he was in his mid-thirties. He didn't mention a wife. He could have a partner. Weddings were going out of fashion in the twenty-first century. She and Paul had been an item. Parting had been civilised. Split the merchandise and wave good-bye. Yet the trauma seemed as hurtful and messy as divorce. Never again for her! She was a free agent. No ties. *That* had been her New Year's resolution.

'Will you have dinner with me tonight?'

Jorja's brown eyes widened in her oval face and pink lips parted, but no words were spoken. Instead her heart thumped against her ribs and butterflies flittered in her stomach. 'No … thank you. I'll just have my diary. It's time to go back to the office.' She sprang off the seat like a jack-in-the-box and held out her hand.

'Hey, I didn't say I wanted *you* for dinner. Do I look like a cannibal?'

'Of course not. It's just that I'm not into dating … period.'

'That bad was it? Join the club. Mine left me at the altar.'

Jorja was stunned. She and Paul had skirted round marriage talk, but jilted, that was really sad news. 'I'm sorry to hear that, but the answer is still, *no*. May I have my diary, please? I'll be late if I don't go now.'

Karl stood and took an oblong black book from his jacket pocket and placed it in her palm. 'See you around, sometime.' He walked away in the direction he had arrived.

*

Jorja's Saturday began like any other weekend, the luxury of an extra hour in bed and a leisurely breakfast eaten at the table. Then the doorbell rang. The long slender box held twelve pink carnations with a card. She read, *I will pick you up at 12 noon, Karl.* The surprise brought a glow to her cheeks then they reddened with anger. What did he think she was? An easy pickup sweetened by a few flowers? He would get an unanswered door. In fact, she needed groceries, which is where she would be at noon.

She hunted for a car park space. There were queues at every till and negotiating the roundabout, dodging manic drivers, left Jorja sorry she had come. Just to avoid facing Karl Bennett! Cowardice had reaped its reward.

Back at the apartment block she pushed the lift button. At the fourth floor, using her back to prop open the door she slid half a dozen plastic bags into the corridor. The pinging frenzy of the lift mechanism deadened the footsteps and two masculine hands picked up the bags.

A hot dishevelled Jorja looked up at Karl Bennett; cool, fresh and groomed - the exact opposite to her. 'May I carry your bags, ma'am?' He was laughing at her. Not out loud. Just that smug-man-thing-versus-silly-woman-thing.

Jorja wanted to say, thank you, I can manage, but it would make her look more stupid than she already felt. 'I live at number 16 … oh … you already know that.'

Inside her kitchen, she asked, 'Would you like a coffee before you leave?' That would put him in his place, she thought. He had managed to manoeuvre his way into her apartment with the bags, but he needn't think it was an invite for the night.

'I'm not an ogre, Jorja. The flowers were a gift, nothing else. Why did you leave me knocking at an empty apartment?'

There was something in his voice that made her look at him.

'How do you see me - friend or foe?'

Jorja needed to be honest; this man had faced one let-down, he didn't deserve another. 'I'm sorry about today, but I'm not ready to get cosy … with anyone.'

'I'll take a rain check on the coffee. Put your shopping away. I'll let myself out.'

The door latch clicked shut.

Jorja sighed and two teardrops splashed onto a plastic bag.

The desk was a shambles and Jorja flung files aside to reach the phone.

'Jorja Philips, Graphics Design.'

'Very efficient, Miss Philips. You make me hesitant to ask you out for a park lunch?'

'Karl … persistent Bennett suits you. OK. Chicken sandwich and a Coke. See you at 12.30. Must go.' She dropped the handset back and smiled, two could play at no choices.

In the park she sat relaxed, reading a magazine, waiting for Karl. When he arrived he stopped a few feet from the bench and she looked up and gave him a welcoming smile.

'That's a start for a friendship, Brown Eyes. I love your smile.'

Over the next few weeks, their park bench lunches became regular dates.

Karl tried several times to ask Jorja out at the weekend, but she held firm to her resolution. One Friday, as they parted, he said, 'I'm away on a business trip to Holland next week. I'll be in touch. See you.' He was gone before she could say goodbye.

Her weekend started as normal, but as Saturday slid into Sunday, Jorja became reluctant to face Monday, knowing that if she went to the park for lunch, she would sit alone. Why had she let herself look forward to Karl's company? Become involved. Laughed at his jokes and listened to stories about his work and walks across the downs. How foolish she had been to refuse his invitations.

Seven lonely days dragged by.

On the Monday, Jorja waited for Karl's call. It didn't come.

Each day when the phone rang, she pounced on it like a cat after a mouse, but it seemed Karl had become the invisible man. On Friday, just before leaving, she picked up the phone and dialled his office and was told he was not available. Well, it was the brush off she deserved, but it didn't stop her heart breaking in two.

She lay awake that night watching the clock tick past two, three, four o'clock. As the dawn chorus chirped the sun above the horizon, Jorja let the tears fall, as they never had when she and Paul had parted.

Saturday shoppers bustled round Jorja with enthusiasm. They seemed to be the happiest people alive, compared to her misery that deepened by the hour. What had she done to make Karl reject her? Or was his trip the excuse he had been waiting for, to end what was a fruitless affair for him? Was he so shallow that he couldn't see she needed time? Time for what? Play with him like a puppet? Lead him up the aisle; then abandon him?

Her mind in a turmoil, she wedged the lift door open and slid the grocery bags into the hall.

Two tanned hands picked them up. 'Carry your bags, ma'am?'

Jorja jerked up and burst into tears, blubbering, 'I thought you didn't want me,' and threw herself at him.

The bags fell to the floor and he hugged her close. 'At last! I've waited weeks for you to thaw, Ice Lady. You're the only person I know that has kept a New Year's resolution going for more than a few days. I'll see you don't make any more this side of the next twenty years.'

'Is that a proposal, Karl Bennett?'

'Half a proposal. We need to spend much more time together before we make it a whole. Starting with dinner tonight.'

Jorja pulled away from him. 'Hey! How do you know about my 'Anti-Man' campaign?'

'Your details are opposite the January 1st page. I couldn't resist a look.'

'Karl Bennett ... you ...' Brushing away the tears, she smiled, 'I need to make one more entry,' and she snuggled into him again. 'Diary lost and love found in the park.'

Julie

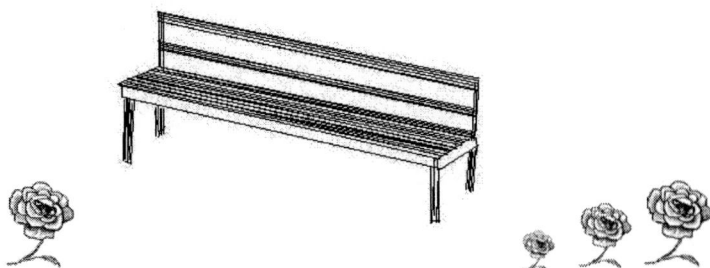

THE GUILTY SUITCASE

'*Guilt!*' *cried Eileen, 'Oh, my poor mother!*'
'*Oh dear,*' *said Vera, 'I'm sure you did your best for her.*'
Eileen waved her glass at the four other women and looked around the room in The Unicorn. She leant across the table towards them and whispered: 'No, no. It was nothing like that. I wish you could have met her; she was a most unconventional woman. She thought nothing of trespassing onto private property if the fancy took her, "We're not doing any harm," she would say.

'I was leaving home for the first time to take up a job as a school matron; I was only seventeen. We went by bus from East Grinstead to Crawley to buy me a suitcase. We had two hours to find, buy and get the next bus back. In a department store we found just the thing, light, capacious and only thirty-nine and eleven.

'Could we find an assistant? There was not one in sight. I looked at my watch, we would have to leave soon or we would miss the bus and have a two hour wait. "We'll have to leave it, Mummy," I said.

"Nonsene!" She picked up the suitcase and started to stroll out of the shop.

"No! Put it down, Mummy!"

"Certainly not. If they can't get the staff organised it serves them right."

Later, in the bus, she said, "We won't tell your Father. And it does give you more money to spend on clothes."

Every time I look at that suitcase, shafts of guilt pierce me - unlike my mother, who never suffered from that emotion.'

The Promise

James Mackenzie was twelve years older than Sarah and she was in love with him. At the start of their three year affair he had extracted a promise from her.

'If anything happens to me while we are together, you must walk away. Jane does not deserve the anguish it would bring. It is bad enough that I've fallen in love with you and this alone has meant a diminution of my attention to her. You do realise that I will never be able to marry you?' He reiterated, 'I'll not leave Jane and the boys. She is a good woman.'

And *I* am a very bad one, she had acknowledged to herself, but had immediately replied, 'This is enough.'

At the time, she had laughed, 'I do think you're being very melodramatic, darling, I fully intend to stay with you whatever the consequences.'

'Then we finish this at once.' She faced him across the bland desert of the hotel bedroom while he outlined to her the possible outcome of their liaison. His low-toned Edinburgh voice was severe and uncompromising, and she already knew enough of him to know that he was immovable. And so she had accepted, although not with good grace.

'Well, I think you should inspect the ceiling in case of unprecedented falling plaster,' she had thrown back at him.

He had poured them both a glass of wine, and moving over to her on the bed had said, 'I really thought that it should be you who would do that. Inspect the ceiling, I mean.'

They had met at the company sales conference and immediately clashed. Sarah had been appointed to the Art department at Lockharts to inject fresh ideas into their rather staid and traditional line of greetings cards. James Mackenzie, the Marketing Director, had opposed her appointment, seeing no need to change a brand that had been successful for over fifty years. They argued over lunch, over drinks and later over dinner, much to the delight of their colleagues who were running a book on how soon she'd be out. A week later they were in bed together.

Sarah had accepted the fact that he would not leave his wife and marry her. Obduracy was one of his attractions. She had since tried relationships with other men, and though enjoying their company would shy away from attempts at anything more intimate. James came down from Edinburgh at least once a month to attend board meetings at Head Office in London and Sarah would join him in the hotel that his secretary booked for him.

Here, at The Tower Hotel, with the lights shining out over St. Katherine's Dock, the inevitable happened.

'James - my dear fellow, fancy running into you here; no idea you were down in The Smoke! And this is ...?' A florid man in his mid-forties was standing by their table. They hurriedly withdrew their hands which had been touching over the tablecloth.

James immediately rose and held out his hand. The man smiled, and his eyes travelled over Sarah, knowing and assessing. 'Tony, good to see you. Allow me to introduce Sarah Forbes who is transforming the image of Lockharts as we know it. Sarah, this is Tony Pardew, who I sometimes allow to beat me on the golf course at home.'

Sarah faced him coolly, but realised that the man had seen their intimacy. She also knew that James had used the words *at home* to show that there were no secrets between them, and that this was indeed a genuine business dinner.

'Well, won't keep you any longer than needs be. I can see you've got serious things on your agenda. Jane, well is she?' he added as he moved away.

'Perfectly, when I left her this morning, thank you,' replied James tightly.

After this, he had told his secretary that the company should economise, and they stayed at large anonymous hotels which would be unfrequented by anyone they might know. Occasionally they went to the theatre, but usually preferred dinner and each other's company. Of his wife they never spoke, although he talked about his sons with pride. Much as she loved him, she recognised the need to build a shell to protect herself. This was why she never invited him to her flat. The nearness of him there afterwards would be overwhelming on those sad, down days when the futility of their situation swept over her.

One evening in June, they had just finished a meal at Wheelers when James put his hand over hers.

'Thought I should tell you, they've detected a spot of angina,' he said with elaborate carelessness.

'You can't have angina in spots, silly,' she said, for something to say, while her world crashed in pieces about her. 'I mean, are they sure? Oh, darling, I am so sorry. What does it mean for you and work and ... everything?'

'Well, if you think it's going to get you out of going to bed with me, you're wrong,' he replied. Then in a softer voice, he said, 'It's perfectly all right, Sarah, everything is under control. I've medication and, with regular check ups, it will make no difference to anything.' He added, 'My brother-in-law's a heart surgeon at the Royal Infirmary so I'm well looked after.'

This was news to Sarah and instead of comforting her, only brought it closer how much of his home life she could not be a part of. So his wife's brother was a surgeon? Would they all meet up for cosy family lunches and discuss his heart? But, loving him as she did, she gave no indication of how she was feeling. He now said, 'You should know that with you I feel the greatest sense of peace and homecoming. That when I am with you, all will be well and there is nowhere else I would wish to be. No one else I would rather be with.'

Greatly moved, and to hide her pleasure, she blinked and said, 'Gosh, sounds as though I should climb into my bunny-rabbit pyjamas and woolly bedsocks.'

'Nothing wrong with bunny-rabbit pyjamas. Bet they're pink. Anyway, you told me you never wear anything in bed.'

'Well, only sometimes if it's cold. And wrong again, they're blue.'

And so, another small minefield was negotiated in the obstacle-strewn path of their mutual lives.

His flight from Edinburgh had been delayed, and by the time he reached the hotel, it was too late to go out for dinner. James was cold and drawn, and also, for the first time since she had met him, he looked his age. Outside on the Hammersmith Broadway, tyres swished on wet roads, but inside the hotel was warm and they dined in the French Bistro. Plastic vine leaves and artificial grapes climbed over the improbable arbours; a waiter came and lit their red candle. There were very few people in the restaurant and she hoped that the steak and red wine they ordered would warm him.

'There, doesn't that feel better already?' she asked, almost as if to a child.

After the wine he seemed to relax, and she teased him that the garlic dressing may have put him off her forever.

'How easy that would be, but how improbable,' he replied.

Afterwards, they went up to their room, where she ran him a warm bath and laid out her overnight things. They never needed to ask which side of the bed was preferred; who would use which towels. He knew that she needed small areas of privacy, and she, that he always sat down on the bed to wind his watch before going to sleep. From the bathroom she could hear the taps being turned off and a splashing sound as he lowered his six foot frame into the inadequate length of the bath.

'That's what I hate about these cheap places,' she heard him call out, 'never enough room for two.'

'Don't worry, I'll come in and make it up to you in a minute, I promise. Got to get approval for the new card designs somehow!' She undressed to her bra and panties, and, sidetracked for a moment, started doodling on the pad beside the bed.

Later, she could not remember how long she had been. It must only have been five minutes. She thought he had gone to sleep in the bath. His face was yellow and he was breathing with a rasping sound. Sarah slapped his face; threw cold water over him; shouted. Remembering the pills, she scrabbled in his brief case and overnight bag. She couldn't find them. This could not be happening.

Dialling the receptionist, she shouted, 'Please get a doctor quickly. My husband needs help. It's an emergency!'

'I'm sorry, madam, the hotel does not have an in-house doctor. What is the nature of the emergency?' a tired voice asked her.

'I think he's having a heart attack. Please, please get someone.'

'What is your room number, madam?'

Sarah didn't know and spent precious minutes looking for the room key before she realised that all she needed to do was to look on the outside door. The receptionist told her that she would ring the Hammersmith Hospital which was only minutes away, and that an ambulance would be there shortly. Meanwhile James had slumped a little further down in the bath, but he was too tall and heavy for her to do more than heave ineffectually, so she let some of the water out. He was now very quiet and she could not tell if he was still breathing.

'Please God, let him be all right,' she prayed over and over again.

Back in the bedroom, she saw herself in the long mirror. White face, black hair, white lace. She threw on clothes to await the ambulance, and then realised with a terrible clarity that she could not stay. The promise so lightly given all those years ago must be kept. Cramming her belongings into her holdall, she went back into the bathroom and kissed his forehead. 'I love you,' she said, and softly left the room.

The red stretches of hotel corridor carpet eventually gave out to the fire escape. Sarah sat huddled on the concrete steps for what seemed an eternity until she heard an ambulance siren approaching. And then silence.

No one saw her leave. It was still raining.

Waking from sleep was worse than the reality of her dreams. She went to work. She could not do otherwise, but still did not know if he was alive or dead.

'Oh Miss Forbes, have you heard the news?' The Lockhart's receptionist leant forward over the desk in her eagerness to impart her knowledge. 'Mr Mackenzie's dead. Heart attack last night in the hotel. Isn't it terrible? His poor wife, what must she be feeling? Mr. Soames is meeting her at the airport this afternoon to take her to identify the body. Are you all right, Miss Forbes? Of course, you and him were quite friendly, weren't you? Oh, and Mr. Reynolds wants you to go through the sales forecasts with him as soon as you get in.'

I am beyond tears, beyond crying, she thought, but even now I do not feel guilt. She telephoned the police at Hammersmith Police Station because she realised they would know that there had been someone else with James. Someone who had phoned the hotel reception and then left. Sarah did not care what happened to her, but she knew that she had to do her utmost to protect his family because that is what he had wanted. The police woman actually asked her if she was all right?

'It doesn't matter about me,' she had replied, surprised. 'I do not count at all in this.' She still did not cry, it was happening outside herself. The police told her to phone the coroner and outline the circumstances. The coroner was grateful for her coming forward and said that it would save him, and the police, unnecessary investigation time. Too many people were being too nice to her and she didn't deserve it.

Then, in the middle of the afternoon, she recalled with photographic clearness the small white cardboard box lying on the night table. Her birth control prescription with name and address in black print! For the remainder of that day she expected the telephone to ring, but it did not. It did not ring on the following day, until just before she was leaving, a phone call came from the police. Inspector Parry asked if she could 'Just pop into the Hammersmith Police Station for a chat, nothing to worry about you understand.' She travelled the several tube stops down to where their lives had ended.

'Very hard all this must be for you,' he observed in his quiet Welsh voice. 'Perhaps you'd like a cup of tea?' He paid for the tea from the machine with his own money, and, inexplicably this started the tears that had not come before. 'Thought I'd just clear up a few practicalities which you might be wondering about. Listen, dear girl, we are not the Morality Police, just understand that. Our job is to save people grief if we can without crossing the law. Jane does not need to know more than she need or can bear. Had a word with the hotel like, and they've - er - amended their register. Your little packet here, I took the liberty of removing before she arrived. Thought it best, no need for more tears, is it? Just sign for it if you would, so we can finish all clean and tidy.'

Sarah said, 'I don't know what to say. I didn't think the police did that sort of thing, but I can't begin to thank you ...'

'No need for thanks, Sarah,' he said, patting her on the shoulder. 'But one thing you do need to know. It was a massive heart attack, and there would have been nothing that anyone could have done, given the circumstances. Now you can grieve.'

The memo had been sent round by the Managing Director's PA. Subject Heading: *JNKM's Funeral.*
The funeral of James Mackenzie will take place on Monday 27ᵗʰ November at 11 a.m. at Cramond Kirk, Cramond Village, Edinburgh followed by a reception at the Holiday Inn, Queensferry Road at 11.45. There will be a private family cremation service in between. The family have requested <u>no flowers.</u>
Sarah could read no more.

A pale, watery sun was fighting to appear from the clouds as she stepped from the taxi late on the Monday afternoon. Traffic on the Hammersmith Flyover streamed by overhead, but here by the hotel it was relatively quiet. No one took any notice as she laid the bunch of yellow roses at the side door. It was London, and everyone was about their own business.

The Guilty Suitcase

*

At Cramond, the slight, blond woman scanned the mourners, looking for the girl with whom she had shared her husband, but saw no one. She was disappointed as they could perhaps have talked a little, before going on with the rest of their lives without him.

Eileen

Tittle-tattle

'It just goes to show,' declared the elderly woman, 'they were only interested in singing, not worshipping.'

'If you say so,' replied Polly. She had her son, Ben, to think of and wasn't going to be drawn into an argument about the rights and wrongs of the situation. Besides, if it weren't for Ben she wouldn't attend the services either. There was something about the Rev Archibald Butler she found disturbing. He was amazed that one of the choristers was the daughter of a mere milkman and had told Polly confidentially he wished certain people didn't attend his church. She wondered if he'd understand the tale of Jesus asking the little black boy why he was crying outside the church. When the child told him that they wouldn't let him in, Jesus replied, 'They won't let me in either.'

The congregation had been taken by surprise, a few Sundays before, when the Rector announced that Mr Jones, the choirmaster, had resigned for, as he put it, personal reasons. Rumours abounded. What could these *personal reasons* be? In these days of religious scandals, many parents jumped to the conclusion their child might have been involved. Why didn't the Rector spell it out? Some of the teenagers in the choir seemed to have prior knowledge of what was going on and took a stand. They'd refused to wear their cassocks on the day of the announcement. Instead, they sat with the congregation and proceeded to compete with those remaining in the choir stalls, setting up such a cacophony Polly didn't know whether to laugh or cry. And now they'd voted with their feet and stayed away altogether. Hence the parishioner's comments about their disinterest in the church service itself.

Ben, however, was younger. He wasn't that good at sports but he could sing and he thought Mr Jones was the best thing that had happened to him in his short life. Now he'd walked out; Ben was devastated. He told his mother, 'I don't wish to associate with Mr Jones any more'. Polly told him not to be so harsh without knowing the full story. After all, he'd been an inspirational choirmaster and had worked unceasingly to make the St Leonard's church choir the best in the area. Ben's confidence and self-esteem had grown immensely under his guidance, and this, in turn, was having a good effect on his schoolwork.

Polly was a determined, intelligent woman in her late thirties and if anyone could discover the real reason for the resignation, it would be her. The Rector was less than forthcoming. 'No, it had nothing to do with the children. And I'm amazed that parents would jump to such a conclusion. I'll do my best to reassure them.' And, 'No, it isn't possible for Mr Jones to say goodbye to them.' Apart from telling her Mr Jones's resignation had been accepted by the church wardens, and indeed, the bishop, he'd say no more.

Why would the bishop be involved? Polly wondered, as she walked back to her car.

'Mrs Henderson?' She turned to find a fair-haired young man hurrying towards her.

'You're Will, aren't you?' she queried, recognising him as one of the boys who'd left the choir.

'Yes, that's right. I've come to collect my money and I overheard you talking to the Rector. I can tell you why Mr Jones had to resign.'

'Come on then, hop in and spill the beans,' said Polly, unlocking the car.

He settled himself into the passenger seat and began. 'We think ...'

'Who's *we?*' interrupted Polly.

'Those of us who've walked out in protest,' continued Will. 'It was Miss Manners. You know, she takes choir practice whenever Mr Jones is away.'

Polly remembered how Miss Manners, a dumpy dark-haired woman, would preen herself and flutter her eyelids during Matins, obviously for the Rector's benefit. Her blouses seemed to become more and more décolleté as the weeks went by, although the church was never that warm. In fact, Polly frequently wore her fur boots to church even in mild weather.

'What about her?'

'Well,' continued the boy, 'we think she walked in on Mr Jones snogging Deborah Wilson in the vestry and told the Rector. I caught 'em at it a few weeks ago!' he added, grinning.

Polly smiled. She couldn't believe even their eccentric Rector would expect the man to resign over that. Mr Jones, a good-looking, middle-aged bachelor and Deborah, a vivacious redheaded soprano, were much the same age. Come to think of it though, Deborah had been missing for the past few weeks. Perhaps a bit of slap and tickle in the vestry was to be discouraged but it was hardly a criminal offence!

'So ...?' queried Polly.

'Don't you see,' Will insisted, 'the Rector fancies Deborah too, but he daren't try it on till her divorce is through. So, at the moment, it's adultery. This way Miss Manners has got rid of them both, can take on the choirmaster's job and have the Rector to herself.'

'Well, snogging isn't necessarily adultery.' Polly had a vision of Deborah and Mr Jones - I wonder what his first name is, she wondered - canoodling among the vestments. She immediately thought of *Allo! Allo!* and René with his implausible excuses to his wife when discovered fondling the waitress. Those old TV series had a lot to answer for.

'Try telling that to the Rev Archibald Butler,' continued Will, 'anyway, we think the Rector forced him to resign. Perhaps he hoped Deborah wouldn't leave but Miss Manners knew better.'

'Thanks, Will. I'll get to the bottom of this if it's the last thing I do.'

'OK, Mrs Henderson. See you around,' replied Will, as he got out of the car.

Polly's husband fell about laughing when he heard the tale. Not one to have a good word for the Rector, this was par for the course. '*Judge not, that ye be not judged* the good Book says, so does our Rev Archie think that doesn't apply to him? What sort of an example is he setting his congregation?'

'What would you do then?' Polly felt annoyed by his flippancy.

'Write to the Bishop and find out if he was involved in this so-called resignation. Ask Mr Jones if Will is right. On the face of it, it's *constructive dismissal* but you can't get involved without making it difficult for Ben to continue in the choir.'

As Polly expected, the bishop's reply was non-committal. However, whilst assuring her of his support for Rev Archibald Butler, it did seem that the resignation was news to him. Polly sent Mr Jones an e-mail, telling him of Ben's distress and asking if he could explain the reason for his abrupt resignation. He replied that he had been given no choice but that he was arranging a get-together to thank any of the choir who wished to come and to say his goodbyes.

A glamorous Deborah was there as were Will and his mates. Ben was introduced to the choirmaster from a neighbouring parish, who took a great interest in Mr Jones's praise for the boy's talent. Ben glowed with pride. And yes, of course, he'd love to join his choir. Polly breathed a sigh of relief. With Ben happy again, she would encourage Mr Jones to go to industrial tribunal. The Rev Archie would rue the day he'd listened to Miss Manners' tittle-tattle.

Eve

Ministry of Sound

My brother, Lawrence, sits slumped in the chair opposite me at the dining table. The other guests have moved to the sitting room, feeling replete after our light but hopefully enjoyable meal. I have been attending a cookery course with Prue Leith, and having guests to dinner, once I've mastered the dishes at the classes, has become almost routine. We, my husband Eric and I, had not expected Lawrence, but naturally made a place for him at the table, placing him between the wives of Eric's associates with the company. At first he seemed fine and talked with everyone, but became noticeably quieter as the evening progressed and, towards the end of the meal, appeared to be lost in his own thoughts. He ran his hand through his dark, curly hair, which was similar to mine.

'What's the matter, Lawrence? This isn't like you at all. Is something worrying you? Come on, tell your sister. Don't you like it out in Australia? You seemed so happy when we visited you there last year.'

'Australia is everything I had hoped it would be, and more, Suzie. As you know I came back last week for a meeting at head office here in London. I enjoyed going out, catching up with old friends - until last night, when I met James. He brought everything back – talking about the incident. I feel so angry and ashamed - sick to my stomach. I just don't know what to do – how to put things right.'

'I'll get you a drink, then you can tell me what has upset you so much.' I poured two brandies – *God - what's happened*, I thought.

'Remember when Annelise came to stay that summer with you, five years ago, to perfect her English at the Biarritz Language School?' He gulped his brandy.

'How could I forget? Such a charming girl and so good with the children. Go on.' I was puzzled – *Annelise?*

'Well, as you'll also remember, Annelise and I spent a lot of time together, going to museums, art galleries, the cinema and the theatre. We had a great time travelling on the riverboats up to Windsor and Henley and visiting country pubs, as well as some of those in the city. I shared a flat in Fulham then with old school chums, and we would all hang out there, but Annelise didn't like going to the flat as a lot of drinking went on and she didn't drink much. I really liked her.'

'Yes, I remember, Lawrence. I thought you two …'

'One evening we went to the *Ministry of Sound*, with a group of friends. It had become popular for partying. I'd been a few times when I was at school and as Annelise liked to dance, we thought it would be fun. It seemed noisier and more crowded than I remembered but we danced, changing partners within our crowd. Somehow I got separated from Annelise and when I returned to our friends, I was told that James, David and Sarah had gone back to the flat with Annelise as she didn't feel well. Shortly afterwards the rest of us bundled into a taxi and returned to find the flat empty. Assuming that they had gone back to Sarah's, I went to bed. The next day, Sunday, I came round here to look for Annelise, but the house was empty!'

'Where were we?'

'Eric had taken you all away for half term. I left, but phoned later in the day and Annelise answered. She said she'd stayed overnight at Sarah's, and we arranged to meet at the Royal Academy the following week.'

'Well! Why the concern, Lawrence?' I was puzzled.

'When we met, Annelise seemed different, more aloof and then, a few days later, she flew back to Hanover without telling me. Shortly after that Sarah told me that some valuable jewellery of her mother's had gone missing.'

'I remember that she left suddenly. We received a telegram to say that she was needed at home immediately. Surely you don't think that the disappearance of the jewellery had anything to do with her, Lawrence?' I said, indignantly.

'I suppose I did. James told me that he had slept with her at Sarah's and in the morning she had gone. I was so angry, jealous and upset, I just backed off and didn't bother to contact her and she, in turn, didn't contact me.'

'Why are you bringing this up now?'

'Last night James got drunk and told me everything. He had laced her drink with Rohypnol, the date-rape drug, at the *Ministry of Sound* and had literally raped her when they arrived at Sarah's. And yes, wait for it, James had picked up the jewellery, slipping it into his pocket on his way out of the flat. He sold it through a friend of a friend. James thought it all a joke, saying that Annelise was such a goody-goody he'd decided to take her down a peg or two. I realised what a bastard he'd been, and still is. He's always been arrogant, with a chip on his shoulder, and to think he now has a prestigious job in the City. How could I have been so stupid? Why didn't I keep in touch with Annelise and find out what really happened? I feel ashamed and overwhelmed with guilt.' His voice was full of pain and remorse.

'I always suspected something had happened but Annelise never told me. She married a fellow graduate – an engineer. They have a little boy and still live near Hanover. Eric and I keep in touch and hope they'll visit us next year.'

'Really...?' Lawrence raised his head.

'Oh, Lawrence, you should feel ashamed for not trusting a decent young girl, whom you liked and respected. But we all carry guilt,' I said in a kinder voice, 'even if we are unaware. So put the past behind you. Come on, let's join the others. They'll be wondering where we are.'

He kissed me on the cheek and, arms linked, we went into the sitting room.

Elaine

The Diaries

The wind blew the pages of the diary like washing on a line. Strengthening, from the east, a pale yellow light crept into the sky and the early morning breeze lessened. White pages lay open and flicked over, one by one.

Monday
The queue was endless. Everyone knew that the sausages were 'off the ration' today. There's never enough for all, but I got mine. I've run out of points this month, so everything will have to be without sugar. Thank goodness Mike and Margery get their milk at school. The weather is still very cold and we've run out of coal. I feel like a wound-up spring; this stretching out the food, make do and mend, hand-me downs. God, how did we get to this? Maybe the news will be better tomorrow.

The queue was endless, everyone stocking up for the forthcoming siege. The shelves are now empty. Coming home, my car held such a small amount of shopping: tins, dry-food packets and candles, torches and batteries. All the chocolate was gone. Masud and Shireen will not be pleased. Allah, how did we get to this? Maybe the news will be better tomorrow.

Tuesday
The factory was hectic today. We were down on our quota, because my machine had broken down - again! I couldn't stay on. Mum's on the late shift at the Odeon, so I needed to get home to the little ones. Aunt Gwen usually helps out, but

she's now working on the trolleys as a clippie. I heard today that Cousin Joan has gone to the country to do farm work. I'm so tired; perhaps the news will be better tomorrow.

Ahmed went to work. Musad and Shireen to school. I've stacked the supplies and sorted out the essential clothing. Everywhere there is fear. Who can we trust? No one. Not even our friends or colleagues. The TV is still alive, but the outlook is not good. I'm so tired; perhaps the news will be better tomorrow.

Wednesday
We've been living each night in the shelter, now in the daytime too. I cradle my two children, thankful that they cannot hear the drone of a V1 or the sudden silence before it falls to earth. Why, oh why, must men wage war and leave the women to weep. How I hate this enemy without.

The sandbags are in place; we are barricaded in our home. I cradle my two children, thankful that they cannot hear the whine of a Cruise Missile or know when it falls to earth. Why, oh why, do I not have the freedom of speech? How I hate this enemy within.

The rescue worker dug in the rubble and picked up a diary. Brushing off the dust he stopped to read. It was a woman's. A dark dried blood stain obscured the date - 1944 or 2003? The same result, only a lifetime in between.

Julie

Pandora's boxes

I carried the four cardboard boxes into the sitting room. Valerie sat by the fire, warming her hands. She looked tired and sad. I placed the boxes on the Turkish rug.

'I found these under Daddy's bed, Valerie. They contain messages: it was how they communicated with each other when we weren't here.'

Valerie turned towards me, a reflection of myself: large brown eyes, a long, delicate nose and pale, clear skin. Her butterfly mouth was down-turned, with fine lines drawn from the corners, giving her face an air of sadness. My other half – my dear twin sister.

I sat on the rug and opened the first box. 'Look, each box is dated: they start when we left - when we married - no - there are some before then; they must have been written when we were away with the school.' I thrust a handful of yellowing paper towards her. 'Should we read them? Or should we burn them?'

Valerie took the notes. 'Derek said we should read everything and keep those we think are important. He should know, he's a solicitor,' she said, raising her eyebrows.

'He won't be a solicitor much longer if Herr Hitler carries on marching through Europe. I can't bear the thought of Laurence leaving me.'

Valerie sank onto the rug, spreading a fan of ochre paper over the reds and purples of the carpet. I shivered, got up and pulled the velvet curtains across the French windows to hide the darkening sky.

'We must press on, Nina. We've sorted out the clothes but I don't want to spend two nights here. We must do the paperwork tonight and tomorrow morning. We want to sell the house before Christmas.' She looked at the notes in her hand. 'Perhaps you're right, we *should* burn them. They seem to be about mundane matters.'

'I think I'd like to read them,' I said. 'We might find out how it all started.' I sat down next to her.

She shrugged her shoulders. 'What does it matter? They're gone. How could they have lived like that? Never speaking to each other – using us to communicate.'

I reached across the rug and squeezed Valerie's hand; it lay limp in mine. 'We'll have some tea and spend the evening looking through their notes. We won't go to bed until we've finished. We can take it in turns and read out interesting parts to each other. That should speed things up.'

Valerie sighed, 'I wonder if we'll find the names of any relatives. Who were our grandparents? Did Mummy have any sisters? Why would they never tell us?'

I picked up the first paper, 'Valerie, listen to this.'

March 1924

Dear William,

We must communicate while the girls are away. I hope that you do not mind me using your typewriting machine. I have been practising every day when you have been at the surgery. I enjoy using it. The book of instructions is excellent. I thought this way we could exchange information, almost as though we were speaking. Please answer me. I will not feel so isolated if I know our fingers have touched the same keys.

Your Bertha

Valerie read out the next note.

The Guilty Suitcase

Dear Bertha,
Your typing is very good. Once again you have surprised me, reinforcing
my belief in your unpredictability. However I agree that while the girls are
away we need to communicate. Please keep the messages to household
matters. Do not see this as a weakening on my part.

William

'What does it mean?' I asked. 'Did they hate each other?
When they were older, Mummy would gaze at Daddy when he
dozed off - such a loving look.'

'You can hardly call forty-eight and fifty-six old!' said
Valerie. 'Daddy seemed to age so quickly after she died - he
gave up. Two funerals in the same year ... the grass had hardly
grown over the grave before it was lifted, tossed aside and
now there's bare earth again.'

We worked our way through the papers; some disintegrating
in our hands and often the typing was so faded that we had
difficulty in reading it. I heaped more coal onto the fire.

February 1928.

Dear William
What are we going to do at the weddings? We will have to make some
pretence for the sake of the girls; I am worried that we will embarrass
Nina and Valerie. We have managed to pass it off successfully when
their fiancés have been with us by only one of us being in the room with
them at a time, but this is different. It is driving me to distraction. I
cannot see how we can go through the day of their weddings without having
to speak to each other. Please, for the sake of the girls, set aside your
intransigence. I promise not to speak to you again once the girls are safely
on their honeymoons. Honeymoon – I had a honeymoon - one night. Was
it a honeymoon for you?

Your Bertha

The Guilty Suitcase

Dear Bertha,
I agree. We must not spoil the girls' day. They deserve it – they have never questioned our arrangements. However, when you speak to me, keep your head down - you must not look at me when you are speaking. I will do the same. We can keep apart as much as possible. It will not seem unusual in a man and wife.

William

'Did they speak to each other on that day?' I asked.
'I don't remember them ever speaking to each other.'

August 1928

Dear William,
Please forgive me for writing to you again but I cannot go on like this. The house is so empty without the girls. Although they visit regularly I am so alone. You seem even more distant. Please write back to me. The silence of the house is terrible. The noise the keys make on the paper is like childish chatter. I feel I am talking to you – please talk back to me.

Your Bertha

Dear Bertha,
I too have been lonely since the girls left. I think it's sensible that we should communicate via the typewriter, but please try to curb your imagination. We need to keep the house running smoothly and I will support you in any charitable work that you may wish to take up, or indeed any other interest that appeals to you. Please - no more fanciful images.

William.

'Valerie, she was desperately in love with him, you can tell. He seems afraid of her and her emotions. Why? Most men would give anything to have their wives in love with them

54

after years of marriage ... wouldn't they?' My heart ached for my mother; she had longed to be loved.

Valerie looked disgusted. 'I can't understand it! This was written twenty years after we were born *and* she still felt passionately about him! Are you still passionate about Laurence? Do you enjoy that side of marriage? I can't say I do. It was a dreadful disappointment to me; not romantic at all – huffing and puffing and falling fast asleep, sometimes without a goodnight kiss.'

I was shocked – I didn't say anything.

'There! I've been dying to tell you. Well? What about you?' demanded Valerie.

'I don't want to talk about it, Valerie. That side of life is very personal and Laurence wouldn't want me to discuss our sex life, but I don't feel as you do. I'm sorry if you haven't enjoyed making love.'

'You mean you like it!' said Valerie indignantly. 'How could you? We're identical twins. I thought we'd feel the same way.'

'Why should we,' I retorted. 'We married very different men.'

She stared at me, looking angry and bewildered.

I wasn't angry but a great sadness swept over me. The letters were full of pain and longing and now a gulf had grown between us. I sighed. 'Only one more box and that isn't full.' Heads down, we silently worked our way through the last of the papers.

'Valerie! Listen to these letters! Poor Mummy.'

August 1930

Dear William

Tomorrow I shall be forty years old. It is twenty two years since I held you in my arms. I have waited patiently for you to forgive me, but now I can wait no longer. Please come to my room tonight. We have so little time left. I need to hold you close to me once more. Once more is all I ask. I know I was wrong to come to your room all those years ago but I believed that you loved me and I have always loved you. Please come to me. I love you.

Your Bertha

Dear William,
I waited for you all night but you did not come. I will not plead with you again. I know now that you do not love me and that all these years we have been together have been because of your feelings of guilt and duty - it was not for love.

Your Bertha

'Valerie, I never realised how Mummy felt – it must have been awful for her. Why did he hate her?' I turned to my sister, tears running down my cheeks.

'He didn't hate her. Remember, at her funeral - he was bereft. He kept her coffin in his study; I went in and found him holding her cold, dead hand. He didn't hate her. God knows what happened between them. I can't take any more, Nina. Please let's leave it for tonight. Tomorrow we'll deal with the rest.'

I nodded and wiped my eyes. The room was cold, the fire had faded. We left the yellowing papers, edges curling, strewn over the rug.

I pulled back the curtains; it was raining. The fire was lit and Valerie came into the room with two cups of tea.

'We need to find birth certificates, marriage lines, any bonds,' she said brightly. 'Derek said we need to find them, although the will appeared to be straightforward. Come on, Nina, wake up! This shouldn't take long – Father was meticulous about his paperwork.'

The Guilty Suitcase

I looked resentfully at Valerie; she was fresh and bright, as though the revelations of the previous night had not occurred. I had hardly slept and as I looked in the mirror I saw smudges of tiredness under my eyes and my skin was even paler than usual – I saw my mother's face looking back at me. I sighed and turned towards the oak bureau. Valerie inserted an iron key into the lock.

'Nina, I can't find a marriage certificate. Where can it be?'

'Do you think that was it – they weren't married? One of the notes suggests that she seduced him - she went to his room. But wouldn't he have married her if she had … you know.'

'Become pregnant with us? I think that must have been the reason for their silence. Perhaps he didn't want to get married – resented being put in that position. I don't know – it's confusing.'

I pulled out the final papers from the last pigeon hole. 'Here's something! It's their birth certificates.' I smoothed out the deep creases. 'Here's Mummy's! Her name – Bertha and date of birth.' I stared in confusion at her surname. 'I didn't know her maiden name was the same as Daddy's. How strange!'

Valerie snatched the certificates from me. She stared at them, one in each hand, her head moving from one to the other. She turned towards me, her face full of revulsion and anger. 'Look at the names of the parents, Nina. Look at the names of the parents on the two certificates.' She pushed them into my hands as though they were impregnated with poison and ran from the room.

Valerie called, 'Here's your taxi, Nina.'

'Aren't you coming to the station too?'

The Guilty Suitcase

'I have an appointment in town - to do with the sale of the house.'

'Shall I come with you? I can catch a later train. We must talk about this, Valerie. We must decide what to do.'

'There's isn't anything we can do. It must be forgotten. Please don't speak to any one about it, especially Laurence.'

'We must meet. What shall we do about the letters? The birth certificates?'

'I've told you, Nina. It must be forgotten.'

I took hold of her arm. 'But we must talk; I need to talk to you about it.'

Valerie prised my fingers away, 'No, Nina. We will never talk about it again. We will not see each other again; it's better that way. We will write to each other at Christmas but after today we will not see or speak to each other. When I look at you I see myself. I see a child born out of sin, our parent's guilty secret.' She pushed me towards the taxi. 'Goodbye, Nina. When you write, keep to mundane matters. Nothing else.'

I looked through the taxi-cab window – she stood at the open door, her arms at her sides. I felt a deep sorrow for her and for myself. How precious love is, I thought. Why deny love? My father denied the love between himself and my mother because of guilt. I know that such a love is forbidden, but surely it is better to love than to live a life of misery and frustration. Valerie has forbidden me to show my love for her and she has denied her love for me. Why? It was not our sin.

The taxi driver asked if I was all right. All I want is to be home, with Laurence. He will understand. He will be shocked but I know that he will still love me. But will he understand? Will he feel the same revulsion that Valerie did? Can I risk telling him? Will it have to be my guilty secret too?   *Vera*

DANCING ON THE TABLE

The five women settled around their favourite against-the-wall-table, in The Unicorn for the monthly pleasure of hearing each other's tales.

'Jealousy!' said Eve, 'Whenever I hear that word I think of Frankie Lane singing 'Jezebel'.'

'Is that the one about the devil without a pair of horns?' asked Julie.

'You've got it! I was seventeen and au-pair to a Swiss family. There were two sets of twin girls, separated by another girl, and two adopted Spanish boys – all teenagers or in their early twenties. You can imagine what fun we had!

'We were on holiday on the Atlantic coast of France. One evening we went skinny-dipping in the phosphorescent sea - a group of seal pups trailing green lights over the water. It was a delicious feeling as the water caressed my body.

'Later in a bar the juke box was playing 'Jezebel'. I felt so exuberant, so full of life. I leapt onto the table and danced and sang wildly to the music.'

'Fantastic! What did the others do?' asked Eileen.

'They clapped and cheered!' Eve smiled at the memory, 'That has put me in the mood.'

*'You're **not** going to dance on the table here, are you?' said Elaine.*

'Perhaps later - now I'll read you my story about Jealousy,' said Eve.

Bitter Irony

'It's no good. We haven't the money to do this place up. We're going to have to go.'

'Oh, Mark, not again! Do we really have to leave this beautiful spot? Just look at the surroundings. We can see for miles across the valley. What's happened to all the plans we made? We bought it because there's so much we could do with it and now we probably won't even get back what we paid, it's got so run down.'

Mark took another swig at his third whisky of the evening, 'It's no good, Pat, the business is on its knees; we can't afford to do the place up and I'm not getting any younger.'

You can say that again, she thought. 'No wonder the business has gone down the pan with you drinking all the profits. I do wish you'd talk to Dr Burnley. You've got a real problem.'

'Now, don't you start all that again, my girl. I don't have a problem and if I sometimes have more than I should it's because you've driven me to it.'

'I'm going to bed, Mark. This conversation is getting us nowhere.' Without kissing him she left the room. She was worried. It wasn't just the business in trouble; their marriage was too.

She lay awake for a long time knowing Mark wouldn't come to bed till the early hours when he awoke from a drunken stupor, stumbled upstairs and slumped down beside her. This state of affairs can't go on, she thought. He'd been on about their having to move for ages. The time had come. Obviously he was right. She'd been burying her head in the sand. But moving wasn't going to mend their marriage. She'd had enough.

The Guilty Suitcase

*

'Jill, you do think I'm doing the right thing, don't you?' Pat was sitting in Jill's smart kitchen sipping coffee, whilst her friend peeled potatoes.

'Pat, what else can you do? It's a very big step to have to start out on your own again but we've only got one life so we might as well make the most of it. It isn't as if you have children to consider.'

'Thanks, Jill. What would I do without you? Mind you, I don't know where I'm going to live. The house is in my name but it's virtually uninhabitable. I'm no good at DIY and I've got to get a full-time job anyway.'

'Funny you should say that, Pat. Brian and I were talking about you just last night. He said, "How about us taking on Jill's property in exchange for this place?"'

'What ...?'

'No, hear me out. I know this is only an ex-council house, but Brian's not a bad builder and ...'

'No, no,' Pat interrupted, 'I just can't believe what I'm hearing. You mean you'd be willing to go and live in my hovel in exchange for this place? Brian's made a fantastic job of it for you.'

'Well, yes, but he could do the same up there and your *hovel*, as you call it, has a lot of potential. The sort of challenge Brian loves.'

'Are you sure? I'll have to think about this.'

I've done all right here, thought Pat as she put her groceries away in her new kitchen. The job was working out well and the house exchange with Brian and Jill had gone very smoothly. Living in the valley she missed the view but the house was immaculate and Jill had looked after the little garden. She hadn't seen her friend for a long time and now she was working all week it was hard to get together for those cosy little chats they used to have. Still she'd been invited to their house-warming next month and she was curious to know how Brian was getting on with the building work up there on the hill. She told herself she wouldn't resent the improvements he was sure to have made. She'd be glad for Jill to have a beautiful property in a lovely location.

Or would she? At the back of her mind was a niggling doubt that maybe she'd been taken for a ride over the property exchange and perhaps Jill wasn't such a good friend after all. She'd had to take their word for it that it was a fair deal because she couldn't afford to look for alternative advice. They'd all used Jill and Brian's solicitors. Had this been wise?

The day of the house-warming dawned bright and clear. Pat phoned Jill to ask if she could help with the preparations but was assured everything was in hand and they had caterers anyway. They would wouldn't they, she thought bitterly. She hated weekends. She was lonely. The rumours round the village following the break-up of her marriage didn't help. She was aware the women with partners regarded her with suspicion. None of her new neighbours had invited her to join their circle: swapping baby-sitting duties, arranging impromptu BBQs and supper parties.

As evening approached, she bathed and shampooed her dark hair. She wished she'd been able to afford a new outfit but money was still tight. Looking through her wardrobe she chose her lilac chiffon dress with its asymmetric hem. Much to her dismay it was a squeeze to get into it. Comfort eating, but only to be expected after what I've been through, she thought. She studied herself in the long mirror. Yes, a little on the plump side but still looking good for a forty year old. Next week I'll start dieting properly. If I wear my shrug over the top, it'll cover a multitude of sins. Shoes were a problem. Her pretty evening shoes would cripple her walking up the steep hill to her former home. She popped them in plastic bag, put on her sensible walking shoes and left the house. Jill had asked her to come early so she could show her what they'd done with the property.

Reaching the gate, Pat stared in astonishment. The transformation was incredible. It must have cost the earth to do so much in just six months. Had she really not seen Jill in all that time? The garden was a riot of colour in the early evening sunlight and the house reminded her of properties in those glossy magazines left in doctors' surgeries to make patients feel even more inadequate. Pat read the notice attached to the gate. Jill and Brian were applying for a big extension and a swimming pool. What do they want more space for, she wondered grudgingly? I hope lots of people object. Stop it, Pat. You're being horrid.

She rang the bell. It played *Rule Britannia*. Yuk, she thought. Jill opened the door, and gave her a hug.

'Lovely to see you, Pat. Come on in. Make yourself at home. Oh, that's a funny thing to say,' she giggled. 'I'm glad you've come early. Gives us a little time for a chinwag before the other guests arrive. What would you like to drink?'

Pat chose white wine and they wandered through to the lounge where Brian was relaxing, beer in hand.

'My goodness, what a lot you've done!' she exclaimed, looking round at the gleaming paintwork and muted décor. The lush green carpet surrounded by pale pink tiles mirrored the patio and garden beyond the wall-to-wall windows with their flowing drapes.

'Yes, it's been hard work,' admitted Brian. 'We can't get over the wonderful view from here. It's different every day. I don't know how you could bear to have left it.'

'Beggars can't be choosers', she murmured.

'Come on, Pat', said Jill, changing the subject, 'come and look at my new enterprise.'

They crossed the hall into another reception room; this was decorated as a children's playroom with a frieze of animals round the wall, marching two-by-two towards the large Ark where Noah stood, beckoning them with open arms.

'I've just been registered as a child minder,' she said. 'You know I can't have children myself and this is the next best thing.'

'I'm surprised they took you on. You still smoke don't you?'

'Well, I didn't let on and I'm trying to give up. In any case, I won't be smoking round the kids. What do you take me for?'

They were interrupted as other guests began to arrive. Many of them were Pat's former neighbours. They greeted her cordially enough but she felt she was no longer one of them. Everyone expressed their delight at the changes Jill and Brian had made to the property. They probably felt she and Mark had brought the neighbourhood into disrepute by letting the house become so dilapidated. Doubtless they were glad to see the back of them. It was an awkward evening and she left early, tired and dissatisfied. No one offered to take her home.

She had contemplated throwing a party to celebrate her divorce but when she found the decree absolute on her doormat one evening a few days later, she felt oddly depressed. In any case, who would come? Instead she opened a bottle of wine and sat staring at the document for a long time. She was startled from her reverie by the door bell. And even more surprised to find two police officers outside.

'Mrs Hunter?'

'Actually, no. I'm using my maiden name now I'm divorced. But how can I help?'

'May we come in?'

'Certainly,' she replied and led the way into the living room.

'It's about Mark Hunter, your husband … I mean ex-husband,' the police constable corrected himself.

'What's he been up to now? Dropped dead in the street, I suppose.'

'Well, yes. He has. It was a massive heart attack and he passed away before the ambulance reached the hospital,' the woman police officer said.

'Bugger!'

The officers exchanged glances, 'Pardon, Madam?'

'Sorry, sorry,' she stammered.

In answer to their questions regarding next-of-kin, she gave them Mark's brother's details and they left, still looking bewildered by her outburst.

'Damn, damn, damn!' exploded Pat as soon as the door closed. 'He never could get anything right, could he? If he'd died a year ago, I could still be in our old home and the insurance would have gone a long way towards the refurbishment!'

Eve

Musician's Dilemma

I seem always to have had good fortune. My father was a baker, as had been his father before him. We had an established position in our village twenty-five miles from Budapest. Mother was a part-time cook at the manor on the estate nearby. I was born in 1980, the youngest of four boys, and was allowed to go with my mother when she went to work. Inevitably I used to play with the children in the household and, when a music teacher came to give piano lessons, I was permitted to learn also. The years passed and it turned out that I had a natural talent which, with the help of the landowner, allowed me to gain a scholarship to the Conservatoire in Budapest. I was able to follow this up, as my mother had an aunt living in the centre of the city and she was happy for me to live there whilst I studied my music. She and her husband had a large flat and a beautiful piano. I was also given pocket money, although I never found out where it came from.

The tutor at the Conservatoire had many contacts and so occasionally I performed at concerts in the city and at other venues. One of these concerts, in a public centre, was attended by a Mrs Forrester from England. She seemed very interested in my playing and told me that her brother was involved in music and asked if I would be willing to go to London. My reply was of course 'Yes!' I gave her my details but soon forgot about the meeting. This sort of interest had been shown before and nothing had come of it.

Autumn came and went and I had many bookings for Christmas recitals and private gatherings. Imagine my delight when I received a letter, followed by a phone call, from Mrs Forrester's brother! My tutor at the Conservatoire became involved and before I knew it I was on a plane to London with all my worldly goods in a battered old suitcase unearthed from a store cupboard back at the old home. It seemed fitting that I should have this receptacle to help me on my journey - a reminder - as I was breaking the ties that bound me to the past. I had visited my parents and friends in the village and they were all excited that I was embarking on a new life in another country. They were full of encouragement and advice, although tinged with sadness at my leaving.

I was met at the airport by one of the staff from the Royal College of Music who took me to an international hostel in the centre of London. I relaxed a little after meeting some of the other students, as I found my English and German to be acceptable. Luckily I had learnt German at the village school and later, as a teenager, English from a tutor. Full of confidence I attended the classes along with a number of other musicians from far and wide, also hopeful for their future. Over the next few days, however, self doubt began to creep in as I realised my limitations due, I felt, to my somewhat narrow background and lack of life experience. Not that I had qualms about my talent as a musician or knowledge of my craft – but will they be enough?

As I had very little money, I kept to myself a lot in my spare time, spending most of it walking around London, occasionally going to the cinema. I felt very lonely and began to feel depressed and to think that perhaps I should not have been so enthusiastic and confident. My new world had become not only challenging but extremely competitive and frightening. The fact that I had a number of benefactors – so I had been told – did not really help my feelings of inadequacy. I began to think that everyone was against me. They all seemed to have so much: good looks, smart clothes, cars, money, witty friends, the know-how to get round London, meet influential people or so they led me to believe. And the girls, the ones I was attracted to, had a quiet confidence - that unattainable look. I felt very depressed. What was I going to do with this green-eyed monster rising within me? Never before had I had these feelings of hopelessness.

Easter was coming up and I received a phone call from Mrs Forrester asking if I would like to join her family in Devon. London often became deserted at this time of year as so many people went on holiday or visited relations elsewhere. I took a few minutes to answer and wondered what she wanted of me, but replied grudgingly that I would go. Arrangements were made and along with a multitude of other travellers, I set off from Paddington. The West Country was very different from London: fewer people, a slower pace and everyone I met seemed genuinely interested in me. Welcomed as a friend, almost one of the family, I gradually relaxed and actually began to enjoy myself. We went walking with the dogs, which I loved, reminding me of home, and usually stopped for lunch at a pub. Visits to Bath and Exeter were very interesting and I began to feel more at ease. After all, I came from a country full of history and beautiful buildings and with a rich culture of its own.

Not long after my arrival I was introduced to the family next door and straight away became attracted to one of the daughters who was at Birkbeck College, University of London, reading International and European Studies. Sophie and I seemed to have a lot in common and for the rest of the holiday became inseparable. I went everywhere with her and sometimes with her friends but all too soon the holiday was over and this magical dreamtime came to a close. I came down to earth with a bang. My feelings of resentment returned. Why couldn't I have been born in a free country with wealth and status, free to come and go as I pleased, instead of being born and brought up in a communist state? I was sure that Sophie would go back to Birkbeck and forget me. When I played the piano I became lost in my music; Sophie and many others said they were enchanted – did they mean it?

My hostess, Mrs Forrester, plied me with good food to take back to the hostel and set a date for a return visit a few weeks ahead. She assured me that I was now part of the family and had a second home in the West Country. Her husband, an affable fellow, pushed an envelope into my hand which, when I opened it on the train, to my delight contained three crisp twenty pound notes. As soon as I got back to the hostel there was a phone call from Sophie asking if she could attend one of the Master Classes. I was delighted and agreed to her coming to the first of these to be held the following week. I remember sitting waiting for my turn to play and being very nervous. Then I looked across the audience and saw Sophie, expectancy on her face.

My confidence returned including my self-worth and I felt as I had done at home - in control. In that moment I knew that whatever happened in the future I had done the right thing in taking that important step into the unknown. My jealous feelings had been unwarranted. The fear of people and things unknown had eaten into me, changing my personality, giving me a false outlook on life. The Master Class and those that followed were a success and I received full accolades for my performances.

I was truly on my way.

Elaine

Coroner's Folly

The crematorium curtains closed on the coffin.

Fiona Marshall let 'crocodile tears' run down her face and dabbed her nose with a hanky. The hand that held it had a silver ring embedded in the flesh on her middle finger. She stood up, noticing as usual, that she took up twice the space of anyone else. When had she become jealous of her sister? Probably when she realised how different they were. Over the years, envy had festered into obsessive jealousy. She was free from all that now; she could begin a new life.

The recorded male voice; heavily accented and with a wheezy rattle, said. 'I took your book.' That was all, and the answerphone clicked off.

In the silence, Fiona stood as though carved in stone, her face drained of any colour and her blue eyes full of fear. If the foreign man was the burglar who had entered her cottage a few days ago, he must know her secret. She forced unwilling feet to move over to the cabinet and with trembling hands searched the drawer. The journal was gone. She hadn't reported the robbery to the police, because she thought he had taken only worthless ornaments.

The phone rang and she jumped like a frightened rabbit.

'Fiona. It's the vicar. I was clearing out the dead flowers bin and found a book belonging to you. It has your name on the cover.'

How was this possible? It contradicted the phone call. 'Yes … I lost it a few days ago. Are you still in the churchyard? I'll come now and collect it.'

'Yes, I am. It's a lovely evening; I'll wait on the seat under the oak tree.'

The Guilty Suitcase

*

Fiona was panting when she sat down next to the vicar.

'Thank you,' she said, as he handed her the precious item.

'You're lucky it's my turn for clearing up this week, old Jack Filey's almost blind.'

'Very lucky, vicar.' *Very, very lucky*, she thought, as she put the book in her pocket.

They sat together, quietly looking at the ancient, discoloured headstones with the evening song of the birds filling the air. The vicar sighed and turned to the woman who had taken over Jeffrey Cooper's law practice, 'How is the business going?'

Under a mass of blonde frizzy curls, Fiona grimaced, but her blue eyes sparkled, 'As well as can be expected. Teaching a dinosaur secretary the ways of the space age is taking time, but the clients are coming in. What more can I ask?' Her smile turned the pale face into a picture-book full-moon.

The church bells began to ring.

'Tuesday practice has started. I must go.'

The silver haired vicar limped away, leaning heavily on his walking stick.

Fiona heard the phone ringing as she walked up the garden path, but it stopped before she opened the door.

His voice was there again. 'I've kept the page.' He was playing cat and mouse with her. How long before he mentioned money?

The sitting room darkened and Fiona nestled deep into the settee cushions. She opened the journal and ran a finger up and down the jagged page edge, waiting for another call. She turned on the television, and jumped each time a phone rang from the screen. When she went to bed, she lay awake and

71

plotted ways to flush him out. Dawn was tingeing the sky when the phone finally rang.

'Five thousand pounds, in used fifties, tomorrow.' The croaking voice was so bad she wasn't sure she had heard correctly and shouted, 'What do you want? I can't understand you.' The voice repeated it slowly and ended the call.

So, it was definitely blackmail – big time.

This was madness, but she needed that page back. Payment was the only way. If five thousand was all he wanted, so be it, but if this was the first of many … she didn't have a bottomless pit of cash … pay this time and see what happens.

The following evening she arrived home and saw the answerphone light flashing. There was only one message and his disgusting voice said, 'Put the money on the grave of Henry Fowler. It's in the middle row opposite the oak tree. At midnight. Not a moment before. Go straight home. I will know if you disobey me.'

There was no mention of the torn-out page. How was she going to get it? Would he post it to her, or phone, saying where she could find it? She shouldn't part with the money until she knew, but if she didn't pay what would happen?

In the moonlight, the granite church had taken on a silvery gossamer cloak and the clock hands were almost together on the twelve. The grass was damp and she stumbled over clumps of moss; the tombs' engravings were difficult to read in the penlight, but she found the grave and drew a package from the inside of her coat. She hesitated, reluctant to leave the money without knowing when she would receive the page. Was there honour amongst thieves? She hoped so. Had Henry Fowler been a thief? Would his ghost, if it were around, make sure the wheezy blackmailer kept his word? 'I leave this package in your keeping, Henry, don't let me down.'

*

There was no post or telephone call. Fiona, feeling like a pendulum, swung between hope and despair.

On the third evening the phone rang.

'It isn't quite enough, dearie. My expenses have risen, I need another five thousand.'

The rattling breath raced through her ear channels into her brain. 'I haven't any more money; you've had all my savings. This wasn't the agreement; I want the journal page back - *now.*'

'A final payment, dearie, or I will send it to the police.'

'How do I know you'll keep your promise?' Fiona's head was hammering and she couldn't get enough air into her lungs; pins and needles were stinging her hands and her legs were sagging. She saw black blotches before her eyes.

'You'll have to trust me, dearie. Five thousand, same place tomorrow night.'

Gulping in air, she whispered, 'I need to meet you this time. Be at Henry Fowler's grave. No page. No payment.'

'OK. Until tomorrow.'

The phone line went dead and Fiona sank to the floor, trembling from head to foot.

Wheezy Voice didn't come the next night and Fiona went home feeling both relief and dread. She knew the blackmail ruse was not over. Did he fear her seeing him? That she would recognise him? But maybe she could turn the tables, exert pressure to force a meeting on her terms, a place and time of her choosing – a dark night, a canal lock. As the plan rolled around in her mind the phone rang …

Deep in the countryside, far from human habitation, Fiona stepped from the towpath into the shadow of the bushes. She pulled on a pair of gloves, pushed the leather down tight over her fingers and crossed her arms under the overdeveloped bosom.

A few minutes later, a short figure in a long overcoat approached the lock. Any shape or disability that could identify him was hidden and a balaclava, slit at the eyes, covered his head and face. He stopped by the lock gate beam, twisting his head like an owl looking for a meal.

As she stepped forward a twig snapped and he turned round.

Fiona's hatred for this man spewed out. 'Have you got the page this time?' She wanted to push him now, but she understood the need for patience. It was a lawyers' rule.

He fumbled in the coat pocket and brought out a sheet of paper; handed it to Fiona. In the light of her torch she saw it was the original page. She zipped it into her anorak pocket. 'Have you made copies of it?'

'No. Why should I? Ten thousand suits my needs. I can always find another sucker to fleece.'

Now was the time!

The splash sounded very loud in the stillness of the night. His arms beat the water, he spluttered through his clogged throat and nostrils as the sodden overcoat dragged him down. It was all over in a few minutes.

The moon slipped from behind water-laden clouds and illuminated her face. A smile of pleasure parted her lips and she said, 'Death by misadventure.'

The cottage light shone like a beacon in the darkness. Inside, Fiona sat cross-legged like a Buddha on the king-size bed carefully taping the missing page back into her journal. She smoothed the creases and read the words - *I killed my twin sister.*

She picked up a framed newspaper cutting from the bedside table. It showed a tall, slim woman in a swimsuit. Her oval face was flawless with arched brows above almond shaped eyes. Flowing blonde hair cascaded down over her bare shoulders and seawater sprayed, as she skied behind a motorboat under a clear sky. High rise apartments in the background shouted French Riviera – the models' photo shoot paradise. The caption read:

'Angela Marshall – Coroner's verdict – Accidental death'

Fiona poked her tongue out at the photo. In a spiteful tone she hissed, 'Slim bitch.'

It hadn't been her intention to become a serial killer.

Julie

The Green-eyed, Monster Chrysanthemum

Philip Larch drew back the bedroom curtains; the sun shot in and he quickly pulled them together again so that Nora wouldn't be wakened. He blew a kiss to her slim form under the duvet and tiptoed downstairs, smiling to himself as he planned his day.

The preparations for The Grand Autumn Show were going smoothly; they'd received a record number of entries and Sam Spetchley, the Show Secretary, had displayed his usual efficiency. If the good weather continues the show will be a great success, he thought.

I'll cut my chrysanthemums before breakfast, give them a good, long drink and tonight, when Nora is at her evening class, I'll be able to brush and tweak those petals. A frown replaced the smile. Not that it will do me any good, he thought. Since Geoffrey Saltmarsh came to the village, the "Big One", the Slater Cup, no longer sat on his sideboard. How does he do it? Geoffrey's chrysanthemums were so uniform in size and colour - perfect. Philip shook his head. Jealousy seethed through his system - that cup should be his.

He heard Nora coming down the stairs as he finished laying the breakfast table in the dining room. Her blonde hair was tousled and a turquoise negligée was wrapped around her curvaceous figure. Philip never ceased to admire his wife's beauty and be grateful that he had persuaded her to marry him; he knew his considerable fortune had helped to make up her mind.

'I found this on the mat, Phillip. No stamp. Must be about the boring old show. Late entry, I expect,' she said, raising her plucked eyebrows in disdain.

'Damned nuisance, late entries. Some people have no consideration.' He shoved the envelope under a plate and attacked the toast and *The Daily Telegraph*.

'I may be late tonight, darling. One of the ladies has invited me back for coffee after the class. I told her you wouldn't mind as you would be locked away with your chrysanthemums,' Nora said, sniffing and looking hurt.

Philip swallowed a mouthful of toast and marmalade and beamed at his wife. 'Jolly good. Have a nice time, darling. Can we have an early lunch? I've got to get to the hall for two o'clock to check on the final arrangements.'

Nora glared at him but his head was once more bent over the paper.

Nora was in the kitchen when Philip opened the envelope. He frowned; it wasn't a late entry, it was a letter, an anonymous letter made up of letters cut from a newspaper.

GEOFFREY SALTMARSH IS A CHEAT. GO IN SECRET TO HIS HOUSE AT TEN TONIGHT AND LOOK THROUGH HIS BACK WINDOW.
A FRIEND.

Philip dropped the letter in disgust. Beastly thing. He stared at the words. Could it be true? If this came out it would ruin the reputation of the show. He would have to find out. If he got proof he would confront Saltmarsh and make him withdraw his entries. He would forbid him to enter the show again, on pain of exposure!

Who had sent the letter? Why hadn't they come to see him? Perhaps it was better this way. He thought angrily of the Cup displayed for the past four years on Saltmarsh's sideboard when it should have been his. The bounder!

Nora came into the cool of the flower room, where Philip, tweezers in hand, was examining his favourite variety of chrysanthemum: it had a large, pure, white flower with an emerald-green eye.

'She's a beauty, isn't she?' he eulogised, carefully tweaking a petal. 'And the perfect name – Desdemona!'

'I wish you spent as long on foreplay,' Nora muttered.

'Sorry, darling. Didn't catch that,' Philip said, as he lovingly placed a paper pillow around the neck of the bloom.

'I said I wished you spent as much time and care on me as you do on these silly flowers! I think you love them more than me. Don't forget – I'll be late.'

'Don't be silly, dear. I may not be here when you get back; I've got to see Sam later tonight.'

As soon as he heard her car move away he gathered the equipment for his mission: boots, torch, binoculars (in case he couldn't get close to the house), camera with flash, notebook and pencil, plastic bags to collect evidence. Adrenalin surged through him – it was as good as being in the Territorials again! Supposing Saltmarsh becomes violent? He's bigger and younger than me, he thought. Reluctantly he took the service revolver from the locked drawer in his desk and placed it with the rest of the mission kit.

Geoffrey Saltmarsh lived in a large Georgian house at the other end of the village. The house was surrounded by an acre of land, but from a previous visit Philip knew that he could get into the garden from a lane which ran at the back of the property. He parked his car two hundred yards away in a lay-by. Humming to himself he put on his commando-style boots and pulled on the black woollen hat that he had found in Nora's wardrobe. He hesitated a moment, shrugged, and blackened his face with boot polish. He looked in the car mirror and smiled with satisfaction. I'll settle his hash, he thought.

Philip looked at the luminous dial of his watch: nearly twenty-two hundred hours. He enlarged a gap in the hedge with a pair of loppers he had added to his kit and squeezed his ample figure into the garden. He moved slowly through the camellias and rhododendrons and narrowly missed tumbling into a lily pond. He emerged tense and nervous onto the open area of lawn which led to the back of the house.

Light shone from the downstairs windows. He could see someone in the kitchen. I'm too low down, he thought, I'll have to get up on the terrace. He placed the bag on the grass and removed the camera. He tucked the gun into a trouser pocket, pulled the hat down to his eyebrows and moved like a two-toed sloth towards the lighted windows.

With his hands resting on the sill he carefully raised his head to look in the kitchen window. There was no one there. On a large pine table were several long, plywood boxes, tissue paper spilling from their insides. Filling the rest of the table were tall, aluminium vases filled with long-stemmed chrysanthemums. One vase contained a dozen perfect Desdemonas – bigger than his – they were monsters! Philip was furious; he raised the camera and took several shots. Then he moved towards the sitting room window.

Saltmarsh was bending over a small table pouring a drink into a tall crystal glass; his figure masking a woman who was sitting in a chair opposite him. Philip could see long, slender legs. Then Saltmarsh moved away and Philip saw that the woman was Nora, smiling up at Saltmarsh and accepting the drink. The cad! Not only was he cheating at the show, but he was making love to *his* wife! He pulled out the gun.

Suddenly arms seized him and a bright light shone in his face. He heard Nora scream.

'Got you. Sit on him, Bob. I'll handcuff him.' Phillip struggled; anger and humiliation flooded through him. He recognised the voice – Constable Ivor Bunting. He was turned over.

'Mr Larch! Good heavens, man. What do you think you're doing blacked-up and waving a gun?' The constable looked up to see Saltmarsh and Nora. 'I see. Touch of the Othello's is it? I always took you for a nice, quiet gentleman. Take him down to the station, Bob. I'll see what these two have to say.'

Philip sat on the edge of the bed in the station cell. I'm ruined, he thought. Ruined and deceived. Bob told him they'd had an anonymous phone call to say there was a prowler in Saltmarsh's garden – a peeping Tom. Philip hoped they would believe *his* story. He had the anonymous letter – it was in his pocket. He heard voices; the cell door opened and Constable Bunting entered.

'Your wife's here to see you.'

Nora rushed in. 'Philip, darling. You were magnificent – so brave. To think you would have done that for me! Would you have killed him?' Philip was prevented from incriminating himself as she threw her arms around him and kissed him passionately. Despite the presence of Constable Bunting, he couldn't help but respond to the ardour of her embrace. This was a new and passionate Nora. He started to see the incident through Nora's eyes.

The Guilty Suitcase

*

'So you suspected that Mr. Saltmarsh was trying to seduce your wife?' asked Constable Bunting later.

Philip looked at Nora, who was holding his hand and gazing at him adoringly. He touched the anonymous letter in his pocket. He hesitated, looked at Nora again, and crumpled up the paper. 'Saltmarsh is a cad. My wife is so naïve, she didn't realise what the man was up to.'

'Mr. Saltmarsh is not pressing charges. We found some very interesting articles in the kitchen.'

'Really? What were they?' he squeaked.

'Never you mind, sir. Because of your good name and the respect we all hold you in, I'm going to overlook the incident tonight. However, I think I'll hold on to this gun, if that's all right with you, sir?' Philip nodded. 'By the way, I think you'll find that Mr. Saltmarsh will be withdrawing his entries; in fact I wouldn't be surprised if you didn't see his house up for sale soon. You both better be going home now. Big day tomorrow. I've got to get home myself and see to my dahlias. Good luck for the cup, sir. Be nice to see it on your sideboard again.'

Philip stepped out of the shower to find Nora waiting for him with a large, fluffy towel. She wrapped it around him, her arms holding him tight.

'I really ought to check on the chrysanthemums, Nora,' he whispered.

She looked at him, her violet eyes wide with promise.

'Damn the chrysanthemums,' he said. 'I'll get up early!'

Vera

A Marriage of Inconvenience

Charwell House stood in five acres of prime Oxfordshire countryside. Its lawns rolled down to the Thames where day trippers on passing pleasure boats marvelled at the battlements, towers and crenellations, sometimes envious of the wealthy people living within. Surely they dined off smoked salmon and quails eggs served on precious plate?

Lady Margaret looked up at the roof and sighed. 'We'll need another bucket up here, Freddy,' she shouted through the loft hatchway to her husband below.

The Fourth Earl of Sedgemore, Keeper of the Privy Stamp, Master of the Cordwainers Guild and Heir to Five Rocks off Tyree, swore horribly and blew his nose on a red spotted handkerchief. 'Bloody Hell, Mags, thought you said that blasted fellow had fixed it for good. Bloody well paid him enough!'

'Darling, he only said that it would do for now unless we had a really heavy downpour, which we have. And we *haven't* paid him,' Margaret called down patiently. Really, her husband was the most terrible fool.

'Hmm, just as well,' Lord Sedgemore remarked and shambled off.

'Freddy, the *bucket NOW,*' she shouted at his retreating back, but knew he would choose not to have heard. Lowering her slim frame through the small aperture onto the ladder, she sighed again. Freddy wouldn't know where the buckets were kept, so it was pointless to go on at him. Much better to do it herself which she always found was quickest. They were running out of buckets, she remembered transferring one from Nimrod's loose box to the conservatory last week for

82

urgent running repairs. Nimrod now drank from an old nappy bucket. *Never Throw Anything Away* had been her motto since marrying into the Sedgemore family, and this had proved invaluable.

Most of the rooms were unusable, with damp and woodworm in contest to see which could do most damage. The one public room still in use was *The Blue Room* and this was the main source of income, hired for wedding receptions and the odd concert. It was, unfortunately, directly beneath the leaking part of the roof, and therefore of greatest concern to Margaret. She surmised that a previous hard-up Sedgemore had probably sold the lead flashing, although her present Lord would have neither the wit nor energy to do the deal.

Margaret Seaton had married Freddy, partly as a retreat from her rather squalid single girl lifestyle, and partly to please her parents. She thought they had had a raw deal from their offspring from whom they'd expected so much. Her younger brother Johnny had already done three months in the local Youth Offender's Institution for selling Class A drugs to his schoolfriends. Her father particularly, had taken this very hard, being the respected local pharmacist from whom the entrepreneurial Johnny had sourced his supplies. After leaving home, Margaret had not fitted into the casual sharing of men and clothes that was the norm in the Chalk Farm flat she rented with Tina and Chrissy. Actually the hurtful part was that they never wanted to borrow her clothes, and she was usually left to answer the phone when they had gone out. The shared bathroom dripped nylons and greying panty girdles, and when the phone rang one evening for Chrissy, she answered it with unusual asperity. The man on the other end of the line was unphased by this, and introduced himself as

Lord Sedgemore. He had found that the title usually had the desired effect, before they met him.

A month later they were married. It later transpired that he'd been given Chrissy's number by a Savile Club friend as a quick lay in exchange for a good dinner, lots of red wine and no expectations. He had not expected Margaret. There had been surprise and a great deal of pleasure on all sides. Except that the Fourth Earl had been mistaken in his future father-in-law. He realised, too late, he did not own the Company of Laxo Inc but merely sold its products. This made things equal, since Lord Sedgemore was in hock up to his very grubby elbows. Creditors followed him like shadows, reluctant to lose sight of him. They took bets on how long he could hold out. Freddy had inherited, along with his house and title, the habit of not paying bills unless forced by circumstances or men with shotguns to do so. He simply went on to the next tailor, corn merchant or butcher until they ran out. Little Charwell had a very meagre supply of these willing tradespeople, and by the time of Margaret's marriage to Lord Freddy, his credit was at zero. The possibility of selling up was never to be contemplated by a Sedgemore. Better to shoot oneself first.

Their marriage day was indelibly fixed on Margaret's memory. After the ceremony in the family church in the grounds, a select few had been invited back to the Morning Room where a surly maid slung around inferior Cava and curling sandwiches of indeterminate origin.

Margaret overheard Lady Dorothy exclaim, 'This is Bloater Paste!' as she fastened on one with huge horse teeth.

'And very good too,' her husband added quickly, as the sandwich tray passed swiftly from his outstretched claw. He reached unsuccessfully for a drink from the passing tray but guests had been limited to strictly two drinks apiece. The maid did not return. 'If we leave now, we could be home in time for

Countdown,' he pleaded with his wife and looked sadly out of the window.

Chrissy and Tina had come to the wedding much against their better judgments, but curiosity had got the better of them.

'How come mousy Margaret hooked this Lord from under our noses?' wondered Tina, 'She never went out anywhere.'

'He's very old,' Chrissy said.

'But very titled,' said Tina.

They were both very jealous and felt that it should have been one of them starting out to be Lady Sedgemore. Out of kindness, Margaret had never told Chrissy that it was she that the lonely old thing had telephoned.

'Can't even get sloshed on this mingy booze,' complained Chrissy.

'And there's no-one under the age of sixty to get off with,' said Tina. 'Better cut our losses and hitch a lift with the waiter - he's going back to Oxford station.'

'Please come and see us when we've settled,' Margaret had called to their departing backs as they tottered away over the unkempt lawn to the drive, their high heels sinking into the clumpy grass. She said this out of politeness rather than expectation, and knew that she would never see either of them again. Margaret watched with little regret as her girlhood disappeared with them down the driveway.

Later, at the station buffet and primed with Guinness, the waiter told them that the Sedgemores were bust, but the new Lady Sedgemore 'seemed a good sort', and he wished her well. He worked at The Happy Shopper in the village and knew all the gossip.

Lord Freddy came to her bed very much later that night. He was wearing red and yellow MCC striped pyjamas and his checked bedroom slippers slapped on the bare floor as he approached.

'Look, Mags old thing,' he said, his words slurring a little. 'Think we understand each other a bit now. Not good at this side of things, but I'll want a bash from time to time. Hope you're up for it? The old urges, y'know ...' He rolled off four minutes later, leaving her sore, unfinished and unreasonably angry with herself for expecting more. She blamed the Canada Geese of whom there were far too many mating on the lawn.

The Fourth Earl smashed in the empty upturned shell of his boiled egg, a habit he had kept from childhood. He peered out through the leaded windows at the driving rain slanting across the waterlogged lawns to the river. It seemed to have been raining all summer since their marriage. 'Can't you try cooking those bloody geese, Mags?' he asked plaintively. 'Surely there's a recipe with lemon and garlic or something. Marinades and so forth? Just sitting there, all of them, doin' nothing. On *my* land,' he added inconsequentially.

'Freddy, don't you think that if they were halfway edible I would not have already tried?' Lady Margaret replied. So saying, she banged the breakfast things onto a tray and took them off to the kitchen, several dark and inconvenient corridors away.

Twenty minutes later she was on the phone in the cold little room she used as an office. In a voice now given to persuasion and authority, she convinced the Sales Director of Come Paintballing that her woods were the ideal location for their next season. She then went on to assure Lady Haresfoot of the exclusivity of Charwell House for her daughter's wedding venue. With two events tied up, she allowed herself a mid-day break, and returned to the kitchen for coffee and a cheese sandwich. She picked up a letter that had been lying on the hall table for days. Margaret had known it was there, known who it was from. The bank manager wrote that he *knew* how easy it was to go inadvertently overdrawn and how *easily* oversights could occur. He had very kindly honoured all the payments, but in line with banking laws had, of course, been forced to charge ... He would like her to bring their account into credit as soon as possible. 'You and me both sweetheart,' Margaret muttered to herself. If she cared to talk this over at any time, then he was entirely at her disposal. What I really need, she thought, is the disposal of this crumbling old wreck of a house and possibly ditto husband, but she didn't realistically feel that this would be within banking law remits. She giggled in spite of herself, and went off to pick the last of the lettuce. It would have to be corned beef and salad again. Freddy hated salad.

The *Thames Princess* nosed its way up river on a fine summer evening cruise. Pete and Wendy Flynn looked out over the water to where Charwell House stood square amidst lawns and cedar trees in the late evening sunshine. They watched a woman with a trug over her arm moving across the grass.

'Wish I was her,' sighed Wendy, 'must be ever so lovely living there. Real posh.'

'Nah,' said Pete, 'those toffs, they don't know what the real world's like - born with silver spoons shoved in their gobs.'

The boat moved slowly away up river, so nobody heard the roaring voice or saw a plate of greenery and brown meat being hurled from a downstairs window. Lord Freddy was displeased with his dinner. Lady Margaret dined alone that evening with her library book propped against a pickle jar, and wondered if the rain would hold off for the wedding.

Eileen

BLUE EYES AND YELLOW SOCKS

'Look at the expressions on their faces!' Elaine passed the photograph to the other four women as they sat around the table drinking coffee at the end of another successful meal at The Unicorn. *In the photograph, propped up against a cushion of a sofa, was a baby; she was staring with interest at a man at the other end of the settee. The man, Michael, Elaine's husband and Madeleine's grandfather, was looking with wonderment and love at his granddaughter.*

'I remember when I first saw that look,' Elaine said.

'Yes?' they asked.

'I was in a train, returning home after dancing in 'Giselle'. I was tired, I remember leaning back against the carriage seat, closing my eyes and thinking about the performance: the solo that I was pleased with, the pas de deux that needed working on. I sensed movement about me, people moving in and out of the carriage as the train stopped at a station.

'I opened my eyes, gazing down at the floor. Opposite me was a pair of expensive, shiny leather shoes, attached to grey trousers with knife-sharp creases. Between the two were bright yellow socks. Intrigued, I slowly raised my eyes. Bright blue eyes stared at me, full of admiration and wonderment.'

There was a collective sigh from the others.

Elaine looked at the photograph again, 'Such a kind, gentle, but strong man. I've always had a weakness for yellow socks!'

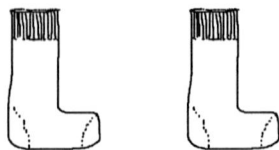

Before Madelaine

Joy means different things to each of us but I can only talk of what it has meant to me. In retrospect, I have been very fortunate to have great joy in my life, sometimes in really simple things, as I suspect most people have.

My first recollection of joy was as a small child in Edinburgh Botanical Gardens, one sunny afternoon, picking daisies and putting them in my straw bonnet. Two young Americans in uniform stopped to talk to my grandparents seated on a bench nearby and, before I knew it, they had picked daisies, so many, and made long daisy chains which they put round my neck and that of my grandmother before continuing on their way. To me this was sheer joy, until I reached home and discovered the fresh-faced little daisies had wilted; a lesson to be learned that joy is often short-lived.

In contrast, going to the theatre to see my first performance of a ballet was the next joy. It lasted from the moment we stepped from the car in front of the theatre, my sister in a dusky pink taffeta dress, myself, in pale daffodil, my mother in blue. We climbed the thick-carpeted staircase leading to the seats, already filling with chattering people. Then the hush as the lights dimmed, the orchestra played, the curtain went up and the stage was filled with dancing figures in colourful costumes. The ballet was *The Nutcracker* and that must have been when I decided that I too wanted to dance.

Lying on the grass in the school playing fields, a few years later, waiting for my turn to play tennis, I had the feeling again on looking up at the sky and watching an aeroplane flying high and then looking down at the field where pewits were pecking for food.

The Guilty Suitcase

The joy of discovering that I could dive from the top diving board at the open air swimming pool at North Berwick, now, I am told, a car park; of walking through woods with friends, crossing the little footbridge over the stream and coming through open fields in the sunlight; after my wedding looking up into the sea-blue eyes of my husband as we emerged from the little country church; looking out over the mountain-tops from Taif near Jeddah in Saudi Arabia, it seemed like the top of the world; sailing on a reach in a dinghy on the Jahore Straits. The first time I went water skiing was a great joy, until I lost my bikini top, to the amusement of onlookers. The arrival of a baby brings great joy - after the birth!

Our children have been a great joy to us and most parents will agree that their children's experiences and achievements bring perhaps even more joy to them than to their offspring. Another joy is sharing my happiness with others.

I have been privileged to attend many weddings and festivals of other cultures, so very different from my own. All have been joyful occasions and bring a feeling of community.

A surprise outing, a meeting with someone from the past, or a small gift can bring joy as can the news that a dear friend has recovered from a serious operation. Standing in the desert, or a snow-covered hillside where perhaps no one else has been, walking along a beach leaving footprints on the untouched sand or looking at the wonder of a spider's web glinting after a cloud burst – all joys.

Our daughter's wedding was a shared joy followed by our most recent and perhaps one of our greatest joys - the arrival of our first grandchild, Madelaine, and then the joyous occasion of her Baptism.

Hopefully there will be many more joyful occasions in the future.

Elaine

Sheldon

Isabelle Courtney looked at the clock on her desk - sixteen hundred hours. It was time to activate Sheldon. She picked up her satellite phone and punched in a code, then dropped it into her travelling bag. Rising from behind her desk, she took her raincoat from a concealed wall cupboard and left.

The rain was heavy as she stepped from the revolving door, but she didn't bother to use her umbrella as she ran up the steps to a waiting monorail train. It was a blessing her Directorate Building was on the National circuit, a train passed every five minutes. Being Friday, most of the seats were taken, but she found a flip-down one next to the emergency exit. She took a hand-held screen from her bag and turned it on. At last, time for herself, she could finish reading her novel. The journey would take two and one quarter hours precisely, the train's speed regulated by how long it stopped at each station.

Muss-by-Weir flashed in red, and Isabelle passed her hand across the halt panel. When the train stopped, the door slid aside and she stepped out onto the raised platform and hurried down the steps.

Sheldon waved, waiting beside a low bulbous car.

'Oh, I'm so glad to see you, Sheldon. It's been a monster of a week. I can't wait to get home.'

'Come here.' He pulled Isabelle close and kissed her on the lips. 'Happy Valentine's Day.'

'Thank you for the celebration trinket.' She lifted her arm and the coat sleeve slipped to her elbow. 'Did you spend all your credit points on me?'

'Who else deserves them?' he said and opened the car door for her.

The ride took only a few minutes and Sheldon parked beside a garden wall. He tapped a code into a screen on his wristband and the house lights blazed from every window.

Isabelle was delighted and silently thanked her ancestors for the inheritance of the twentieth century cottage. There were not many brick and wood properties left. Modern housing consisted of bland and featureless apartments, even in the country.

An hour later, Isabelle looked at her reflection in the mirror as she combed her dark hair and coiled it into a high knot, securing it with a tortoise-shell clip. It had cost a year's worth of working points, but it was something she just had to have. Pulling on a swathe of multi-coloured cloth she belted it round her waist and slipped her feet into soft moon-thread shoes and left the bedroom.

Pausing in the doorway of the dining room, she heard Mozart filling every corner. On the table, laid for two, candles flickered, (but they never dripped wax), and stark white poly-textured plates looked out of place amidst chintz furnishings. Noises came from the kitchen: the pinging of the infra-red oven, the hiss of plastic expanding, and the smell of food. Looking immaculate in a black and white suit, Sheldon came in carrying the dishes.

'I've chilled the wine to your exact liking. It will be a perfect dinner.'

He filled two antique fluted glasses and handed her one. He raised his high and smiled, 'To our last weekend.' Isabelle did not respond, just raised her glass and sipped. 'Shall we eat?' He took her wine-glass and placed it on the table, then pulled back the chair for her.

'Thank you.' It was said with a sigh.

Sheldon served with the expertise of a waiter and the grace of a dancer, and placed her plate in front of her.

He was driving her mad. She gripped the knife and fork like daggers and wanted to plunge them into him. Instead, she said, 'Thank you, Sheldon. It looks delicious. I marvel how you manage to present synthetic trash to look like vegetables.'

'I am a master of all things, Isabelle, you know that.'

Why was he irritating her so this evening? The past year had been wonderful. She worked away for five days and the weekends were to relax. And yet her nerve ends were tingling.

'Make love to me, Sheldon. Now.'

He looked up from his plate, 'But you programmed for twenty-three hundred hours.'

Isabelle wanted to scream, '*To hell with your program,*' but she pressed her lips together and looked down. 'Of course. Later.'

Sheldon got up and came round to stand behind her, then bent and kissed her ear lobe. 'Would you like me to reprogram? I am also feeling a strange urge, my love. We have spent more time together than was originally detailed. In fact, my feelings for you are becoming very human. Is it possible that my circuits are developing emotions?'

'Don't be ridiculous. You're an android. I know that and you know that. Serve the dessert.'

Sheldon stepped back, but there was a little moisture in his eyes, almost like tears.

It looked like strawberries, tasted like nothing.

Isabelle drained her third glass of wine. He was doing it again: folding the cloth with precision, placing the condiments together in a perfect triangle, positioning the chairs as if they had a marked spot on the floor.

'Oh, for heavens' sake, Sheldon, sit down.'

'In ten minutes, Isabelle. That is how long it will take to stack the dishes in the washer.'

She couldn't stand it any longer; her anger with him had become overwhelming. She was losing control. For fifty-one weeks they had enjoyed perfect weekends, what was wrong with her? Sheldon had seemed the solution to her life. She had a career, a thousand credits each month, a city apartment and Sheldon for relaxation.

Programmed Sheldon!

She was so deep in thought, that she didn't know he was there until his warm lips touched her neck.

'Now?'

Isabelle looked at the clock. One minute to eleven.

'No. Go away.'

'Away? Away where? To our bedroom?'

'Yes. No. Wait.'

She turned and looked at him - he was so handsome! She had been extremely selective when she marked the boxes for his features, manners and masculine attributes. So why was she being so contrary? She could pick a new one next week; try out a continental gigolo, a hunk from the outback? But she didn't want to change him. That was her dilemma.

Isabelle rose and went to him. She put her arms round his neck and whispered in his ear.

Sheldon laughed against her neck, 'That is very naughty of you.'

He picked her up and went out through the door.

The March sunshine was warm as they walked beside the river. Hedgerows were showing the faintest hint of green and narcissi were breaking into flower.

'Sheldon, look, there's a nest over in the reeds.'

'Just like last year. This was our first walk together, remember?'

'Yes, I do.' And this would be the last. The thought sent her into a spiral of memories: Sheldon experiencing life with her, enjoying what she enjoyed and storing it away to remember later when they talked and laughed. She didn't want to come here again with another.

'Shall we lunch at The Duck, in the old cellar room? Reminisce about highwaymen and stagecoaches?'

'No.' The cellar was her favourite retreat, but not today. 'The Moon Room. Up-to-date. Perhaps they have a picture of the new Crater Base complex. I hear it houses a hundred-thousand people.'

Sheldon made no comment, but took her hand and raised it to his lips. 'Are you all right, Isabelle?'

'Yes, of course. Let's go and eat.'

The Moon Room was only half full, as most of the clientele preferred the old haunt downstairs.

After the meal Sheldon asked, 'Caffina or Aftersweet?'

There was reproach in Isabella's voice as she answered. 'Sheldon, you know I love the thick syrup drink. After all, you were the one who enticed me to try it. I'll have the green mint, please.'

He ordered two.

After they were served, Isabelle noticed he was fidgeting with his glass.

'You are agitated, Sheldon, do you have a circuit problem?'

He took his hand away. 'No!' His brown eyes looked into hers. 'Time is running out.'

Isabelle could see something in his gaze that she had not expected. Love, desire and pain, all rolled into one. Dynamite exploded into her, piercing her heart. 'Yes. Do you want this to end?' Sheldon did not reply. 'I'm sorry, that is not for you to say.'

'Shall we go? The light is fading and the temperature is dropping. I'll set the fire to come on.' He tapped in a code on his wristband. 'All warm and cosy, in your little antique cottage.'

Isabelle picked up her bag from beside the chair and stood up. 'You sound disapproving?'

'No. Jealous of who will come after me.'

She was shocked by his reply and realised that they were both going through a form of trauma this weekend. What did that mean? What emotional part of him was fighting the countdown, the hours they had left together? Was she jealous of who would have Sheldon next?

'Let's go home.' She didn't want to think beyond tomorrow.

Every Sunday, Sheldon brought Isabelle breakfast in bed at nine hundred hours on the dot. It was set out to perfection on the tray, including one flower, always picked from the garden.

'Is this daffodil real?'

'Yes, but from the glasshouse. I know they are your spring favourite.'

'Old fashioned me. I do love you, Sheldon.' She stopped abruptly. 'I mean, I love your consideration, your ...'

Sheldon turned away and pressed the switch on the wall and the curtains opened to let in the morning sun. 'Another beautiful day, would you like to go for a drive?'

'Later. I thought we might edit our images before I return to the city.'

'As you wish. I will collect them and put them on the oak table.'

Isabelle sensed an indefinable tension growing between them. This made her impatient with him. 'Oh, do stop being so bloody precise. How many minutes is it going to take you – ten point three-three-three recurring? What will the never-ending fraction do to you? Send you up in smoke.' She moved the tray and threw back the covers. 'Sheldon, I didn't mean that, I didn't mean to … Oh! What a wicked thing to say.'

Sheldon reached for her and drew her close. But he did not deny her words.

'Get ready, Isabelle. I'll see you later.'

Isabelle waited beside Sheldon. The early evening sky was clear and the stars resembled sparkling diamonds. A humming vibration sounded, signalling the mono-train would arrive in a few seconds.

'Don't work too many late nights next week. The High Council will drain you dry if they can.'

Work was the last thing on her mind. All Isabelle could think about was next weekend. There would be no Sheldon to meet her, no Sheldon to comfort her and no Sheldon to share her hours with. 'I promise.'

The humming grew louder and she looked into Sheldon's eyes. It was there, again, that explosive dynamite. He pulled her close and kissed her. 'Goodbye.' Then got into the car and drove off.

In her apartment, Isabelle lay awake all night.

At six hundred hours she got up and went to her desk, switched on the lamp and connected into her satellite link system. She tapped in several codes and the screen flashed the form that had been saved for the last year. Her finger hovered over the boxes that said 'retain or return'. Then she touched a box.

She picked up the phone and tapped in a number. Sheldon's voice answered.

'Sheldon, it's Isabelle. Please tap in code nine-zero-zero-nine.' She heard the pinging on his wristband, but not the final voice confirmation. 'Sheldon?'

'Are you sure? Nine-zero is to retain, but adding zero-nine will convert to all human functions. I could be late to meet you at the station; we might quarrel, fall out and not speak to each other, might …'

'Oh, Sheldon, just push the button. What joy! I'll be home in …' Isabelle looked at the clock, 'three hours, fifty-five minutes and nine seconds. Just have the mattress heater turned on.'

Julie

The Memory of Joy

Richard Cleeve stepped out of his 'study' into the trench and called to the nearest soldier, 'Find Sergeant Doggett, would you. Ask him to see me straight away.' The soldier saluted, 'Yes, sir!' and squelched through the mud of the sand-bagged trench.

Richard Cleeve sat down at the small desk and started to write his daily letter to his wife Minerva and their three children.

14ᵗʰ September, 1916
My Dearest Minnie, Roger, Spenser and my little Bessie,
Today I'm writing a special message to each of you. If you wish to share my memories, now or in the future, I would be pleased.
First of all some general news ...

'You sent for me, sir?' Sergeant Joe Doggett, professional soldier for eighteen of his thirty eight years, blocked out the light that filtered down the sides of the trench into the tiny space in which Richard Cleeve was writing. The walls of the 'study' were sandbagged and the wooden roof, protected by more sandbags above, had stood up well to the bombardments.

'Come in, Doggett.' Richard Cleeve pushed a stool from beneath the desk and indicated to the sergeant to be seated. 'We'll be going over the parapet tomorrow morning, as soon as it's light. There'll be a heavy bombardment tonight and before we attack they'll detonate mines in the tunnels. This time I think we'll take High Wood.'

''Bout time, if you ask me, sir. We've been at it three months! We've tried the whole bleeding lot: cavalry charges, gas, flame throwers, mining the Bosch trenches as well as the usual.'

'I know, Doggett, but we have advanced; one last push should see us through.'

'Yes, sir. Shall I tell the men?'

Richard looked at his watch. 'Let them have their tea. Get as many as you can into this trench,' he waved to the outside, 'I want to have a word with them.'

'Going to give them one of your assemblies, sir? I like your assemblies. Wish you'd been *my* headmaster, I might have learned a bit more.'

Richard smiled at his sergeant, 'Over the past two years *you've* been my teacher, Doggett. Without you I wouldn't be here today.'

Doggett wriggled on his stool and wiped his hand over his thick, red moustache. 'Very kind of you to say so, sir. Just hope the young 'uns can cope tomorrow; we've two that haven't seen any action before.'

'It's hard for them,' Richard said, 'they've got used to the bombardments, the lice, the rats and the mud. Now they must climb up over the trench wall and march into enemy fire: every one is a hero. But you've drilled them well, Sergeant, you've made fighting men of them.'

'They'll do. I've seen worse.'

'Muster them for five o'clock.'

'Seventeen hundred hours, sir!' said Doggett, shaking his head.

'Sorry, Doggett, most remiss of me.'

The sergeant hauled himself from the stool, saluted and stepped out into the trench.

The men, crammed together, stood in silence. Richard Cleeve saw trust in their eyes and tiredness etched in their faces. He saw Private Arthur Murray, a fresh-faced country boy, young enough to be his son, staring at the other soldiers. Poor lad, he thought, will he survive tomorrow?

'Men, I have important news for you. Tomorrow morning we'll be making an advance on High Wood. You know the drill and how you must act. Listen carefully for the whistle signals. I know it will not be easy but *you* men,' he indicated the hardened veterans, 'must help the younger ones.

'This evening I want you to do two tasks. First give your rifles a thorough clean and check your kit. The second is not so much a task as a duty, a pleasant duty. I want you to write a letter to your family, your sweetheart or someone you're fond of. Don't dwell on the living conditions or tell them of the horrors of war. Write to them of special moments that you have had together, moments of joy. Then they'll know that you are thinking of them and it'll give them comfort. I have paper and pencils if any of you haven't any. If you are having problems, see me or Sergeant Doggett and we'll try to help you. The Padre has promised to collect the letters tonight. Any questions?'

A tall, thin soldier with a shock of blond hair raised his arm. 'What I want to say to the missus wouldn't be fit for the kids to read. How do I get over that one, sir?' The rest of the men laughed.

Richard Cleeve raised his hand and the laughter died away. 'That wasn't the kind of memory I was thinking of!' There was more laughter. 'I'll tell you what I'm going to do.' He saw their interest sharpen. 'Inside *my* main letter I'm enclosing four separate notes. They won't be long, but I'm telling each of my family of a special memory I have of them, one which has given me great joy. I think you'll sleep better tonight and face what tomorrow brings with a lighter heart if you have thought of these moments.'

'Do you think we're going to buy it tomorrow, sir?' asked the blond soldier.

'We all know what the odds are, men. You've been well prepared and I will pray tonight that we all come safely through. Whatever the outcome, your letters will bring comfort to your loved ones. Sergeant will be round tonight with the rum ration and again in the morning to warm you up before the charge begins. We're ready to do our duty and tomorrow we'll walk out of here and High Wood will be ours!' The men cheered. Richard wasn't sure if it was the rousing words or the thought of the rum.

'Sir. Can you help me?' Private Murray stood in the doorway clutching a sheet of lined paper and a pencil.

'Come in Murray. Having trouble with the letter?'

'Yes, sir. I haven't got a girl friend and I can't think of any joyful moments I've had with my Ma and Pa. Ma doesn't say much and Pa works hard in the fields and just sucks on his pipe after we've eaten. I fight with my younger brothers and my older sister's married an' lives away. I write for my pocket money and ask them to send me comics.'

'I see. Tell me what do you like most about the farm?'

Arthur scratched his brown hair, which sprouted from his scalp with all the exuberance of spring grass. 'I loves the animals most, specially the cows. I likes to go down to the meadow on a summer morning, with the mists rising and call to them. I have my own special cow, she's called Mildred. Pa's promised to look after her 'til I get back.'

'That would be a good thing to write about to your parents, Murray.'

'Would it? Why, sir?'

'It would show them that you loved your life on the farm and that working with the cows gave you joy. Knowing that would make them happy.'

'I see. Well I also likes ploughing and ratting. Wish I had my Spot here, sir, she'd see to those rats, she would! I could write about that, couldn't I?' he said, looking much more cheerful.

'Splendid! You've done well, Murray. Good luck for tomorrow.'

'Thank you, sir. Same to you!'

Richard Cleeve wrote the letter to his wife last:

My Dearest Minnie

I shall never forget the first time I saw you. Your father had invited me to your elder sister's birthday party. It was at the end of my first year teaching classics. Your father had been kind and helpful to me and later, when I first became a headmaster, I tried to model myself on him.

There were about twenty youngsters as well as people of your father's and mother's age group. I remember there was music, laughter; it was all rather hectic for me. I wandered into the library and seated at the open window, reading, was the most beautiful, dark-haired girl. She had a solemn face as she concentrated on her book. I said, 'Hello. Who are you?' She looked up and a luminous smile made her even more beautiful. 'I'm Minerva. You must be Richard Cleeve. My father has told me about you.'

I was in love. Instantaneously and for ever. As the years have passed my love for you has grown different facets: lover, wife, the mother of our children, but I can still feel that intense joy when I first saw you. Minerva, the wise and beautiful girl, reading her book.

I hope to return to you and the children.

Your loving husband,

Richard.

The Guilty Suitcase

*

Sergeant Doggett came into the 'study'. 'Signal should be going up soon, sir.'

Richard Cleeve nodded. 'Hell of a bombardment. Hope it's blown Jerry's wire to shreds. How are the men?'

'Quiet. Determined. I think writing those letters has made them want to get on with it. Finish the job. What made you think of that, sir? You haven't done *that* before.'

'I remembered a quotation, some Greek philosopher: "There is no pain so great as the memory of joy in present grief." I decided I didn't agree with him. I believed remembering joyful, happy times can only do us good. Now I'm not so sure, perhaps he was right.'

'Reckon you're right, sir. I thought of downing a pint of mild and bitter. Lovely. Couldn't think who to write to about that, so I just imagined it going down my gullet, nice and slow. It cheered me up no end.'

The guns had stopped their bombardment. The first signs of dawn paled the night sky. Richard Cleeve put on his helmet, drew his pistol from the holster and stepped out into the trench. The men were crouched at their posts, rifles ready. It seemed to Richard that all the air had been sucked from the trench and he felt, as he always did before a battle, unable to breath.

A signal lit the sky. He turned, 'Ready men? God go with us.' He calmly climbed above the trench, waving his pistol for them to follow. It was time to go for a walk.

Vera

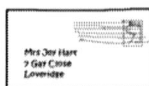

104

Give Me Joy …

Emma was devastated. *He's only twenty-four; too young to die.* Jack had been diagnosed with cancer soon after their marriage, which began with a wedding day best forgotten. Money was tight. It was a quiet affair at his village church with just a dozen or so friends, no bridesmaids, no bridal gown, a few white roses and a cake from the local bakery. Emma, tall and elegant, wore her best dress, her long dark hair swept up into a becoming chignon. Jack's pale grey suit seemed too big for his slight frame. Her mother, Doreen, refused to attend. *Mum knew just how much hurt she was inflicting,* thought Emma bitterly, *hadn't her Congregational parents stayed away from her Catholic marriage ceremony?* His mother came reluctantly and made it very plain she was not happy about the union.

Now she was accusing Emma of being the cause of Jack's cancer. 'Well,' she surmised, 'he didn't have it before you two got together. Stands to reason you gave it to him.'

It had taken Jack a long time to realise he wasn't going to recover. There were quiet times spent at home with Emma in their small rented flat, and longer periods in hospital with mother-in-law and wife avoiding each other. Emma had left the job she loved on the farm to work as a shop assistant just to be near the hospital. They'd had such plans and been looking forward to owning their own farm one day; to having children and being a proper family. Now Jack was dead. He was at peace at last, but she was still haunted by his eyes pleading to understand.

She choked back her tears and read the letter again. This uncle she'd never met had invited her to come to America and enclosed the airfare. She was welcome to stay with Uncle George's family for as long as she wished. What was there to stop her? What had she to lose? She'd lost the love of her life.

Her mother, whilst commiserating, urged her to *move on*. 'I don't want to sound callous,' she'd said 'but it's a blessing you haven't a baby to hold you back.'

If only, thought Emma wistfully. George was her father's brother, and although her parents had been separated for many years, George had kept in touch with the family.

With a heavy heart and full of apprehension, Emma left for Florida. Welcomed with open arms by George's large family, Emma slowly came to terms with her grief. Although she never wanted to sit behind a desk, preferring the outdoor life, she learned to type and in time found work and a small apartment near her uncle's home. She resisted his efforts to convert her to Catholicism but found faith, joy and comfort at an American Protestant church. Several years passed before she and the preacher fell in love.

Hank was ten years older than Emma, not a well man and a divorcee. They married despite Uncle George's vociferous objections. He valued his Irish Catholic heritage and divorce was not to be countenanced. Emma had followed her heart again and wedded against the wishes of her family. Once more, it was not a white wedding, none of their relations attended and they had to be content with the good wishes of Hank's congregation.

This was to be another short but happy liaison. Soon after the wedding, Hank's church sent him to Montana where Emma and he worked together to help alcoholics and drug addicts. It was hard work but the rewards were beyond their expectations. Hank's congregation grew and raised funds for a larger church. Celebrations to commemorate its opening were well in hand, when Hank collapsed and died in Emma's arms.

In her grief, she found consolation in her faith and the friends they had made.

With their support she managed to earn a living and eventually bought her own home. Gradually she took on more responsibility in the construction firm where she worked. She even took a few holidays in England visiting friends and family but had no desire to return to her homeland permanently. She was saddened not to have had a child of her own but after much heartache and many tears she vowed she'd get on with the rest of her life.

She thought wryly that, in the unlikely event she met someone new, she'd check his medical record before she got too involved!

If there were to be a next time she wanted it to be before her fiftieth birthday and she'd have a white wedding with all the trimmings. There was Joe, of course; a big quiet man with a soft American accent who visited her office more often than was absolutely necessary. He was a construction engineer and had summoned the courage to invite her out twice, but she'd been reluctant to accept. She'd had two happy if brief relationships and was apprehensive about starting a third. On the other hand … third time lucky …? Perhaps Joe felt the same? The next time he asked her out she accepted.

Joe was a widower with three children, the youngest of whom was just seventeen. They took to Emma immediately, loving her English accent and the joy she exuded to everyone around her. Joe and she found great delight in each other's company. Two months before her fiftieth birthday, dressed in a long white gown, she stepped from her stretch limousine and, surrounded by Joe's children, glided serenely into the chapel to Wagner's *Bridal Chorus from 'Lohengrin'* to be greeted by a smiling Joe in his well-cut tuxedo. Her heart missed a beat. This was her dream come true. The piano began playing

her favourite hymn, *Give me joy in my heart, keep me praising …*
Yes, she thought, things can't get better than this. Thank you,
Jesus. How have so many sorrows culminated in such joy?
This wasn't what I planned for my life but I'm happy to go
along with it.

That life-changing day happened almost twenty years ago and
here they were preparing to celebrate another anniversary of
loving joy surrounded by their children and grandchildren.

'How blessed we are, Joe,' she murmured

He hugged her close, 'Yes, Emma, we've had our
challenges. But with your help, those three rebels of mine have
come up trumps and we all love you very dearly.'

Eve

The Vicar, The General and The Girl

My father had devoted his life to God and the Church of England. Unfortunately he was also devoted to drink and women, and as these were incompatible, the Church threw him out. We don't know what God felt about it.

I think my mother had looked forward to this catalyst so that she could join her estate agent lover of many years. *He* certainly would never be short of a house or two. She rushed off to him with never a backward glance, and only the scantiest advice about changing my knickers every day and defrosting the fridge. Never wanting children, she was not a natural mother and openly admitted to 'having children thrust upon her.' Literally!

My two brothers, Gregor and Ralph, were away at boarding school, and missed all the drama. Aged twelve and fourteen, they were ideal boarding school material, and thrived on uncomfortable living and rough outdoor games with balls, sticks and guns. I loved being at home and I loved it even more when they were away. And now I had my handsome father to myself.

We had been bundled out of the Rectory with indecent haste, Father's latest indiscretion being prominent in local society. It turned out that it was not so much what he did, but what he did *not* do.

'Bloody woman! Told her I was an ordained priest and wouldn't dream of divorcing my wife. The very idea.' He looked outraged as he related this to me, 'Don't you dare turn out to be a harpy, Joy, then I really will feel as though I'd failed as a father.'

In my sixteen year old wisdom, I had to agree with him. Throughout our childhood, women had appeared at the slightest excuse to arrange flowers, iron surplices and bake cakes. And lingered. I really don't know how my mother stood it. Yes I do, she had The Lover.

Following his fall from grace, Father had been offered a job as gardener with a tied Lodge on the estate of General Hardwick. They had both been up at Trinity together; Father had gone into the Church and Johnny Hardwick into Warfare. Although poles apart by nature, this arrangement worked ideally. My father - the now *not* Reverend James Albin - apparently saw no loss of stature by this downturn in his affairs. Indeed, he seemed far happier than he had done for years. The General would drop in for a glass of whisky or two on his way back from killing something, and I would lurk in the background breathing in the heady smell of wet tweed, alcohol, dogs and leather.

Better for me at school too. At one stroke I was no longer the Vicar's Daughter, but a person worthy of attention having lost a mother to Interesting Circumstances. I went to the local comprehensive because my father felt that private education was wasted on girls, and my mother wasn't interested. The school suited me very well being large and anonymous; a child sent to report to the Head for a misdemeanour could be gone for days. There were indeed days when I simply didn't go at all.

My appearance helped. I was tall with grey eyes and fair hair which I thought made me look ethereal, misty. My brothers called me 'mooney.' Same thing, different little boy words. I had make-up hidden in a drawer, but didn't wear it because I was saving it for a special time. I was scared the first time I put it on because it made me into another person that I didn't recognise. An older, street-wise siren. I say 'hidden,' but the secrecy wasn't necessary as it would be with a mother snooping around. My father didn't pry, though I sometimes wished he would. He didn't realise I was growing up. I went into town by myself and bought my own first brassiere. It was called *English Rose* and had lace and a pink bow to keep my breasts apart - well no, of course it didn't keep them apart, but it was in the middle of where they would be eventually.

The lady in McIlroys Corsetry Department asked, 'Is your mother not with you, my dear?'

'I am afraid she was called away on urgent business,' I lied. I did not want anyone knowing my mother was no longer on the scene and feel sorry for me. 'I will take it. No, I will take two, please.' One on and one in the wash. Did I hear my mother say that or did I invent it, hoping that she did?

Later that week I had come home from an evening prowl, and peering into the lamplit room, saw my father and the General seated across from each other by the fireside. Two men, heads bent together in the firelight, hands clasped round heavy crystal glasses, smoke and malt mingling in the heavy air. With a shock I realised that here was indeed another handsome man.

'Don't lurk about in the darkness, dear thing,' my father called out, 'come and say hello to our Benefactor.'

It was obvious that my father and the B had enjoyed more than one glass of whisky. I came further into the room and stood in front of the General. My outstretched fingers briefly touched his, and I saw the sudden shaft of interest as he lowered his eyes to my breasts. I was wearing the *English Rose* bra to try it out. Not just the daughter of a friend, but now, a young woman.

I realised then that this was how it should be done.

I don't tell anyone my plan. I know that in order to keep my father close, I need to marry the lovely General, and then we can all move into Hardwick Manor together. Certainly they have already shown their pleasure in each other's company, and the only woman that will be needed then is me, as a backdrop. Of course, I have to get him first but if I wear the Make-Up and the *English Rose* bra it should be enough. I will have to get better knickers - or panties - than my white Aertex, for the first time, but after that I can go back to normal. But in the long run it's my father he'll prefer and I can keep all the sex bits down to a minimum. I do wonder what it would feel like to run my hands through his thick, iron-grey hair? His body is certainly hard from weary campaigns. There are other bits that I don't know much about, but I am sure that we can work that out. Oh, I have forgotten my brothers. Well, that will be all right because they can go on living in the Lodge when they come back for the holidays. They don't mind where they live. Anyway, they'll probably want to go on Commando courses and the General can help them with that. Already I feel proud of what I will achieve for them.

I heard somewhere that an army marches on its stomach, so the General will expect to be fed well. Our food at home has admittedly been hit and miss since mother left, so I need to learn how to cook. Later of course, we'll get a Cook.

I go to school and at the small Home Economics class I am greeted effusively by the teacher.

'Joy, how unusual to see you in my class, but welcome nevertheless. Today we are cooking *Easy but Impressionable Dishes*, to get you through ghastly evenings of His Boss and Wife. This is not down on the curriculum as such, but you will thank me in times to come. Joy, are you sure you want this?'

'Oh yes, Miss, that is exactly what I want.'

The Guilty Suitcase

My father has certainly seemed to enjoy the creative and economic meals I have been producing for him. Lately though he has been leaving some of them - like *Pilchards with Fried Sippets* I've cooked from Paul Hamlyn's *One Hundred Cheapest Meals*. But I wouldn't cook that one if the General was coming. He does not visit as often as he once did. I think he is afraid of the sexual *frisson* that passed between us. I can understand that.

My brothers are home for the Easter school holidays and have brought a friend. His name is Jon Wright and he is tall and fair with blue eyes. His family are in Hong Kong so he can't go out to them this time round. They have invited my brothers out for the summer. He tells us his parents own the fourth leg of a racehorse that they run at the Hong Kong Race Circuit. I'd love to watch it race. I cook for the boys and it's fun. They have improved by being away, or else we have all grown up a little. Jon and I go for a walk on our own and he says that I must come out too. He holds my hand. I cannot tell him my plan and feel a twinge of regret. Pity we have no money for fares to Hong Kong, besides, I don't think the General would like his wife going off like that. I am beginning to have doubts about all this.

General Johnny Hardwick is bankrupt and is selling the Estate and moving into Our Lodge. My father accepts this with his usual grace and optimism. God and he work in very mysterious ways but my father never seems put out by God. I am glad that I have not told him about My Plan.

Father is starting work on Monday with Gardens Is Us. The pay is fine although the grammar is not, but I'm sure he'll change that. And so we will all have to change accordingly.

Realistically, the General has hairy hands which I do not think
I would like.

Eileen

THE MOON IN A TENT

It was the end of October and the quality of daylight was so poor, even at mid-day, that it could have been early evening. The blazing fire and friendly atmosphere at The Unicorn were comforting. They ordered their meals and gathered around their favourite table.

'This is just the weather for talking about fear,' said Eileen.

'And just the right time of year, it's nearly the thirty-first,' said Julie. 'I remember when I nearly frightened a poor child to death at one of my Halloween parties.'

'You didn't take your mask off, did you?' said Eve, 'Sorry, only joking!'

Julie shook her head pityingly. 'Every Halloween I gave a party for my son, and most of the children in his class. The year he was nine I decided to take them on a journey to the Moon and a tent was put up in the back garden; this was to be our Spaceship. On the invitations the children were told that they would train to be Space Cadets; the parents were asked to dress as aliens, but not to let their offspring into the secret.

The children, in track-suits sat on cushions in the tent and watched an old movie made in 1904 – Journey to the Moon. Then Holst's The Planets' boomed out and they were told to close their eyes and the music would guide them to Moon Base.

The adults crept in: I was dressed as The Academy Principle in a gold cloak ...' she paused as someone's wine went down the wrong way! There was Darth Vader, a monster in an old gas mask, another in a red fright-wig and other incredible aliens.

'A little voice near me whispered, "Have we landed? Can I open my eyes now?"

The Guilty Suitcase

"*We have landed on the Moon. Open your eyes!*" *I declared. The children gasped as they saw the motionless aliens all around them. The music from '2001, A Space Odyssey', filled the tent and the aliens came alive: first their eyes moved, then their arms reached out to the children and their heads gyrated around their shoulders. The little girl next to me screamed and cringed.*

"Don't tell the others," I whispered, "they're not really aliens."

Later the children carried out different tasks so that they could qualify as Space Cadets. Surprisingly they all passed and were presented with certificates!

When the 'Space Cadets' were tucked up for the night, the aliens, still wearing their costumes, had a party of their own.'

Phobia

The only splash of colour on the pale corridor walls were framed prints of the countryside and evenly spaced teak wood doors, each with a single nameplate.

Behind one of these, the sun shone through a high barred window onto a man sitting in a legless, rounded upholstered chair; his thin frame bent beneath hunched shoulders. The hiss of the hydraulic door made him look up and he registered his surroundings: in the ceiling a single, round opaque light, that was never turned out, and cream-cloth walls buttoned at intervals. His eyes searched for the hidden door and, as it opened, a broad figure in a blue striped dress entered carrying a tray. The man drew his legs up under his chin and hugged them with long-boned fingers. He dropped his head so that he didn't have to look at the giant ant walking towards him, with its smiling black face, spiked dark hair and large, spectacled eyes.

It spoke, 'Medicine time, John.'

The hypodermic needle pricked his skin and black claws pushed the plunger down and then caressed the hole in his arm with a swab. A black-jointed hairy arm encircled his shoulders, cradled him into its soft belly and a claw brushed the thin grey hair from his forehead. He struggled to free himself from its suffocating warmth, leapt from the chair and scrambled under the plastic framed bed. The door hissed open and closed. He was safe again.

The ants had started annoying him when they were babies, their little black bodies scurried back and forth from a crack in the concrete outside his back door. They marched in rows through the flowerbeds, circled under the shed, in and out of the rock plants hunting for food. They had grown bigger. They climbed the shed door and disappeared inside, stealing minute pieces of wood shaving. He had swept them off with a broom, sprinkled killer powder, even burnt them, but still they marched, day after day after day.

They got bolder; the military lines came over the doorstep along the hall skirting into the kitchen. They grew fatter and fatter on his jam and sugar; stronger, so that he couldn't push them away. And they grew even bigger. They crawled up the stairs, into his bed. They wanted him. They wanted his flesh, his eyes and his brain. He had tried to fight them off. Finally, he ran into the street, but they clung to him, clawed him down into the gutter. Frantic with fear he had cried out for help.

It was the postman who saved him; wiped them away.

But one had followed him here; the one who came in, bloated with food, and jabbed him with poisonous needles.

A regular pattern of daylight followed by darkness passed the barred window.

He heard the hiss of the door. Fear ran through him like a torrent of water breaking a dam; a pain started in his chest, he felt hot and his mouth went dry.

The mutated ant came towards him pushing a wheelchair. The legs and arms had become human and as it helped him from his chair, he noticed it had fingers with creamy nails. Ant-woman still grinned and spoke soothingly, hypnotically. 'Don't be afraid, John, we are going for a little ride to say 'hello' to the other patients.'

They went along a corridor and swing doors opened. Ants of all sizes turned to look at him. They were all here; they had come from his garden to claim him. He twisted in the wheelchair, raised both hands to cover his eyes. His mouth opened and closed, but no words came out, although his mind screeched, No! You can't have me.

'Come, John, turn round and let me introduce you. They are harmless - believe me.'

He squirmed and dribble ran down his chin. Lowering his hands, he opened his eyes. He saw people. Human people, knitting, reading, playing cards – ordinary people – but he was still afraid. She wheeled him amongst them; one touched him, placed her warm hands over his cold ones, but he was glad when he was taken back to his silent, safe room.

It had been a trick; they were coming for him out of the walls. First the one with the clicking needles, then the card player, its fan of cards like a barbed spearhead. He flung himself against the wall, hitting out with bunched fists, head-butting them between the eyes. He kicked at their legs until they faded back into the padded cloth. He had fought his demons with body and mind and was victorious. He would not let them invade his life again.

The door hissed. The ant-woman had gone and Sadie had taken its place. 'Good afternoon, John. How are you today?'

His wall of silence stood firm as he watched the dark-skinned nurse with large, red-framed spectacles walk towards him. Had he been so ill that he thought her an ant? Foolish man! Yet, he couldn't speak to her; it was as though his voice box had seized up, like a broken motor-engine.

'It's time to see your Doctor. Will you walk and then visit the Lounge on the way back?' He nodded, 'Fine, off we go.'

The weeks of care showed. He straightened his shoulders and got out of the chair. Flesh had thickened over the thin frame and he linked his arm through Sadie's as they walked out into the corridor.

*

He moved to a new room with green walls and a carpeted floor, although it still had a barred window. He felt trusted because they didn't lock the door and he could walk along the corridor to the Lounge. He didn't see them now as ants; but as human puppets without strings. Like the skeletal man in striped pyjamas, who moved slowly and shuffling, always with a blanket round his shoulders, a mimic of an emaciated prisoner of war, while another man jumped around like a sprung pogo stick. He never spoke to anyone, just sat and watched.

His final step towards recovery was when he walked from the confines of the hospital into the garden. A breeze lifted his hair, rippled across his face and his eyes watered with joy. Across the lawn were oval flowerbeds of Busy Lizzies and dahlias, and perfume carried from the rose arbour. Gardening was his hobby, more than that, his life's pleasure - until the ants had appeared. Were they here? He began poking his finger around the plants; he couldn't see any. Good, this gardener had them beaten. Tense and wary he sat with Sadie on a bench and cried.

His bed was made and the room was bare except for a small holdall packed ready for his return home. Strange feelings were stirring in the pit of his stomach, his heartbeat quickened as thoughts of the outside world crowded in, but he fought to hold them down. Everything would be all right; he was in control.

Sadie walked with him to the taxi; patted his hand as she said goodbye.

In the sunshine his front garden looked neat and tidy. The hallway smelt fresh, the kitchen spotless, every shelf washed clean with new pots of jam. He went upstairs and stopped at the closed bedroom door, his hand shook as he reached for the handle. Someone had been busy on his behalf; there wasn't even a dirty sock to be seen.

Back in the kitchen he plugged in the kettle then opened the backdoor - and froze.

They were there, waiting for him. He had told that hook-nosed doctor, over and over, the ants were after him, *only him.* Panic made him go dizzy and his hands tingled with pins and needles. He sank down onto the floor as they marched over the doorstep towards him.

The shrill of the doorbell penetrated his senses, but his body felt like stone, too heavy to move. It shrilled again, this time longer. He rolled onto his side and crawled to the newel post at the bottom of the stairs and pulled himself up. Again the bell, this time it rang continuously.

He reached the door and fumbled with the latch and Sadie came in.

His stricken stare told all. *'What's wrong,* John?'

Mute, he moved to the backdoor and pointed. They were not there, just the late summer sunshine on the brightly coloured flowerbeds.

MYRMECOPHOBIA - Fear of ants

Julie

The most frightening experience of my life

English Homework for GCSE Folio – Rough Draft (*Work in progress?*)

November 3rd.

I'm the youngest of six children and my name is Danny. I'm fifteen years old and I'm going to take my GCSEs in May. I'm writing this because our English teacher, Mrs. Edwards, who we all worship, (*the guys anyway*) has set this subject for our homework. Well, Mrs Edwards, listen to this!

I was ten years old and it's only now that I'm mature that I can reflect on the frightening events and bear to tell what happened. It will be a good experience to reveal the trauma that I went through as a child as I intend to be the first teenager to win the Booker Prize. To achieve this goal I better start writing soon, as I've only four years left and I'll need to find a publisher as soon as I've written the novel.

I was a right little toe-rag. (*Would miscreant be better?*) I was perpetually in trouble at school and at home. I felt misunderstood by my parents and teachers - I was only expressing my childish high spirits.

It was spring, the rising sap and swirling winds sent me on a trail of destruction. My Mum, who had to deal with the complaints from school, was a regular visitor to the Alma Mater.

There was the incident when I tried to thin everyone's hair when the teacher was out of the room. I had observed Aunt Audrey demonstrating her newly acquired tonsorial skills on my Mum and I thought that several of my class mates – especially the girls – would benefit from *soigné (learnt that in French this week)* hair styles. The teacher was not pleased when she returned to find half the class in hysterics (*girls*) and the other half laughing their socks off (*boys*).

The incident which led to my seventh suspension was when I persuaded Alice Walker that she would go up in the estimation of the class if she performed a strip-tease at break behind the bike-sheds. I provided music on my ghetto-blaster and collected contributions for charity in my cub cap. Poor Mum, she was so ashamed of me, she hated going to school to sit in front of the Head Teacher and be told off.

I didn't learn, and because of my high intelligence and vivid imagination I proceeded to instigate one bizarre event after another.

Then I went one step too far. I had been watching *Masterchef* with my parents. They fancied themselves as *bon viveurs* and invited their friends round for noshes at which they consumed strange foods such as sushi, polenta and balsamic vinegar, (*don't like it on chips!*). I was impressed with the programme, especially the flame thrower for burning the tops of puddings, and I liked the wild atmosphere that the dinner parties engendered. I could see there was a lot of mileage in the Impression Stakes here, and so when a suitable opportunity occurred I invited a few mates around for a taste of the good life. My parents had gone round with the other five children to Gran's. They deposited me at football training but I sneaked back - I knew where a key was hidden.

When you're ten you're not very tall. Have you noticed this? It's difficult coping with a frying pan and a wok ring when standing on a kitchen chair. The fire was only a small one but the water damage was considerable as we used the garden hose to put out the fire and it did lead to a water fight. But I think my mum was really upset because I'd used up all the virgin olive oil. I had noticed, even before the kitchen disaster, that she'd been grumpy and short-tempered for about a week.

Well, when she saw the mess she went off her trolley - she went into the stratosphere!

'I could kill you! You obnoxious, poisonous little bastard. I wish I'd never given birth to you! You are the most vile, disgusting child ever born.' (*Call me Damien! No pocket money this week.*)

Despite my cool exterior, I must admit I love my Mum - still do. I was feeling pretty sad that she hated me so much.

Dad gave me his withering look, shook his head and muttered, 'IQ 160! How can this be?' Dad and I had not yet got into male bonding.

This had started Mum off again - this time at Dad. I was sent to my room. Much later, after all the other kids had gone to bed, I decided to nip down for a choccy bic and a gulp of coke - luckily the fridge was still working! I could hear my parents muttering in the living room. I knew they would be talking about me, so I crept to the door and listened.

'... but it would be murder, it really would, there is no other way to describe it ...' That was my Mum.

Mutter, mutter, mutter.

'... but as the youngest in a large family, there will be so few material ...' My Dad. Mutter, mutter, mutter.

'... We must think of the other children ...' More from Dad.

Mutter, mutter, mutter.

Help! They were planning to kill me! I knew that I was terrible. I had seen all the other mothers stare at me and pull their Rodneys, Shauns, Liams and Erics to their bosoms and look pityingly at my Mum. I knew I was crazy – but this was murder!

The next day, at play-time, I told the guys of my discovery.

'I can understand it,' nodded Eric wisely, 'I'm surprised they haven't done it before.'

'Can I have your Action Man when you're dead?' asked Shaun.

'They must have got religion,' said Liam excitedly. 'You know, when God told Abraham to kill his son?'

'We'll have an assembly for you, and a memorial; perhaps an annual football tournament on the anniversary of your death,' enthused Rodney.

'Great!' they all said in unison.

That was it. I decided that the best thing to do was to beat it before everyone joined with Mum and Dad in removing me from this planet.

I didn't get very far; managed to avoid being found for a couple of days and was discovered by a lady jogger under a park bench on the third morning. She was lovely, nearly as nice as Mrs Edwards, with big, soft breasts which I snuggled my head into. I lisped a bit, sucked my thumb and did my David Copperfield act. (*Dickens – not that old magician.*)

Mum folded me in her arms and Dad kept scraping the top of my head and making choking noises. I had to admit my cool crust was in tatters and I was having a good old sob.

'Danny, Danny. We love you. I love you, Danny. Please promise me that you'll never do anything like this again,' said Mum.

'But you were going to kill me! I heard you and Dad talking. I came downstairs and I heard you say I was the youngest, I was awful and that it would be murder. You wouldn't murder one of your own children, would you? *Would you?*'

I felt my mother's body become rigid. Her head jerked up as she looked at my father. Wrapped between them, I watched as they looked intently at each other. It was like the X-files.

An eon of time passed; then my mother lowered her head and looked into my eyes. 'No Danny, we wouldn't murder one of our own children.' The words were said slowly and with great emphasis, and as she finished the sentence, she raised her head and looked defiantly at my father.

'No, Danny,' he said, 'we'd never do that. We love all of you. We'll always love you whatever you do, whatever the sacrifices. You are all, every one of you, worth all the worry and anguish that you have and will give us.' He seemed to be speaking more to my mother than me; but I appreciated his words. He leant down and kissed my Mum. She smiled, tears pouring down her face and they enclosed me in their mutual embrace.

Wow! Was I really this important? It was then that I decided not to be a stumer and to use my intellectual powers for the good of mankind.

A few weeks later they told me, with the rest of the family, that Mum was going to have another baby. Great, I thought, if they get wobbly again they can get rid of this one instead of me. Hope it's a boy; we need a left wing to complete the team. It was only after I learnt a few more things about babies that it became clear.

Of course the baby was a girl. She's a right pain and all her little chums like to come round and drool over me. One day I may tell her this story and how I saved her life. But perhaps not. I don't think she would like it.

I know what it feels like when you think your parents are going to kill you. I don't think I'll give this piece in for my

GCSE folio. I'm not sure what Mrs Edwards would think. She'd probably want to refer me to the school shrink; or the police would come round and arrest my parents for abusing me. I'm not sure you can really trust teachers.

Vera

Great Aunt Bertha

It was the summer holidays and Jemma and Elizabeth resented being sent to visit Great Aunt Bertha. She was tall, skinny, old and grey. Her ice blue, bottle-bottom spectacles were ugly and she smelt of mothballs. She expected to be kissed whenever they met and the girls found her soft, sallow cheeks repulsive - even worse were her wet lips when she kissed them. Once they'd seen her without teeth, her lank hair hanging round her face. Sometimes she didn't seem to know who they were or asked them about relatives long dead and unknown to them.

Every week they visited Bertha with Nancy, their mother, but today was the first time they were making the journey on their own. It was only a bus ride from the village and a short walk from the bus station to the narrow street of Victorian terraced houses where Bertha lived.

Climbing the steps to the front door, Elizabeth lifted the knocker and banged it down several times. They waited a while and then she tried again. Nobody came. Jemma peered through the front window but the heavy net curtains made it impossible to see inside. She tried the door. It opened and a marmalade cat shot out between her legs. Jemma squealed and Elizabeth began to laugh. 'You looked so funny …'

'It's not funny,' retorted Jemma, flicking her pigtails. 'Why's the front door open? Do you think something's happened to the old bat?'

'How would I know? You'd better go in and have a look.'

'Why me?'

'"Cos you're the oldest, of course.'

'I'm not going without you.' She grabbed her sister's hand and gingerly pushed the door open. 'Aunt Bertha!' she called tentatively. No reply. The girls tiptoed into the dark linoleum floored hall. The door to the sitting room was closed. Rather than open it, the girls went through the open kitchen door and put the cake and pie their mother had made on the dresser. A teapot and two cups and saucers stood on the draining-board. Jemma felt the teapot. It was still warm.

'She can't be far away,' she announced. 'Pr'haps she's in the loo.' She glanced out of the kitchen window at the outside lavatory, the door was open and it was unoccupied. 'Must have had someone round for a cuppa this afternoon before we got here.'

'Well, where is she then? Do you think she's gone out without locking the front door?'

'Maybe. We can't let Mum know 'cos there's no phone here. Let's take a look round, then we can go home,' Jemma decided. Carefully she opened the hatch between the kitchen and sitting room. In the dimness, she could make out the overstuffed armchairs with their grimy antimacassars, the occasional tables covered in crumpled lace cloths, the clutter of ornaments on the mantelpiece and the dark pictures scattered on the walls; but no Aunt Bertha.

Hearts pounding, they cautiously climbed the steep stairs. Elizabeth couldn't remember ever going upstairs before. Both bedroom doors were closed. They looked at each other. 'Let's open them both at once,' suggested Jemma quietly.

'OK, you first.'

'No! No, you do that one and I'll do this one at the same time. Are you ready? One, two, three …' Jemma turned the handle but the door stuck. Elizabeth's burst open and she nearly tumbled. The room was full of boxes, cases and old furniture. She turned to help Jemma. 'Who's there?' a man's voice called. Without hesitating, the girls bolted downstairs and out into the bright warm sunshine.

'Now what?' gasped Jemma.

'There's someone up there and it's not Aunt Bertha,' spluttered Elizabeth.

'Clever clogs!' said her elder sister scornfully, then, 'There's a phone box on the corner; let's give Mum a ring. She'll know what to do.'

Nancy was not pleased when they rang. She was relaxing in the garden reading her book, enjoying the peace and quiet without the girls. She sometimes found it difficult to cope with the two of them on her own. After all, she visited Bertha every week; surely she could have one week off?

'Stay where you are,' she told them. 'I'll have to get the car out and come and find out what's going on.' With that she sighed and hung up.

The girls wandered back to Aunt Bertha's house and sat on the front door step. There was no way they were going back inside. One or two people walked by and glanced in their direction but no one spoke to them. Then Aunt Bertha came into view! She was tapping her white stick on the pavement and muttering to herself as she flapped along in her bedroom slippers. They leapt to their feet and called to her as she came near. She leaned forward peering at them through her thick glasses.

'Who are you and what are you doing littering my doorstep?' she demanded. 'Be off with you!'

'Aunty Bertha, you know us. I'm Jemma and this is Elizabeth.'

'I certainly do not. Off you go!' She waved her stick menacingly at them. They dodged out of her way and ran up to the corner of the street.

'She's gone dotty,' panted Jemma, 'but Mum should be here soon to sort things out.'

*

The old Ford Popular trundled round the corner and pulled up in front of the house. Jemma, frequently interrupted by Elizabeth, explained to Nancy that Aunt Bertha had come back but was very agitated and didn't seem to recognise them. Oh no, thought Nancy. For some time she'd been concerned that her dear old aunt, the last of her generation, was becoming increasingly confused; she'd been trying to find a suitable old people's home for her.

'Well, let's go and see if she knows me,' she said, more cheerfully than she felt, 'and solve the mystery of the locked room. Bertha!' Nancy called as she opened the front door with her key.

'Oh! Am I glad to see you! I've had a dreadful day and I'm so frightened. There's a man upstairs. He keeps shouting and knocking. It's terrible.'

'Hang on a minute. I'm just coming.' Nancy yelled up the stairs.

'Well, hurry up! I've been here at least two hours,' a male voice shouted back.

'Now, Aunty, come and sit down and tell me what the trouble is.' She took Bertha by the arm and guided her into the sitting room, settling her in an armchair.

'Well, Martha, I went out but I couldn't remember why, so I came back and now I'm very tired.'

'I'm not Martha. I'm her daughter, Nancy. You know me, don't you?' she said this gently, but didn't remind her that Martha had died three years before.

'You look familiar; but don't let those horrid girls in, will you?'

'They're my daughters, Jemma and Elizabeth. Don't you remember?'

'No! Don't let them near me!' cried the old lady, visibly shaking.

'You just sit there quietly then, and I'll try and sort things out.' Telling the children to stay in the kitchen and not to disturb their aunt, Nancy went upstairs and tried the back bedroom door.

'Who's there?' called the man's voice again.

'I'm Miss Huggins' niece. Who are you?'

'Thank God!' he exclaimed. 'I called to read the meter and collect the money. Your aunt asked me to come up here to change a light bulb and she locked me in. Can you let me out?'

'She's taken the key away. I'll see if I can find it.' Nancy went down to the sitting room where Bertha was slumped in her chair asleep. Quietly, she picked up the old lady's handbag and went into the kitchen. She explained to the children who was locked in the bedroom and they both doubled up laughing; their relief obvious. Nancy told them to quieten down and make a pot of tea, whilst she looked for the key to let the poor man out. Amongst the old envelopes, Christmas cards, out-of-date diaries and other rubbish in the bag, she found the key. Jemma and Elizabeth looked at the growing heap of useless objects in amazement.

'Why does she keep all that stuff?' queried Jemma.

'Oh, don't ask me,' replied her mother tensely, 'Aunt Bertha probably never empties her bag.'

Climbing the stairs again, Nancy unlocked the door. 'I'm so sorry,' she said as the harassed, good-looking man emerged.

'Don't worry,' he replied, smiling. 'I meet all sorts in this job. This isn't the first time I've been taken for a thief.'

'What do you mean?'

'Well, once she'd locked me in, she told me she was going to look for a policeman, 'cos I'd stolen her savings from her moneybox. All I did was collect the shillings from the meter.'

'Oh dear!' sighed Nancy, running her hand through her dark hair, 'What a mess. Come down and have a cup of tea. It's the least I can do. And thank you for being so understanding. I think I'd better take my aunt home with us for now.'

Hearing this Jemma groaned and Elizabeth said, 'Does she have to?'

The man winked and Nancy smiled at him. Pulling herself together, she said, 'That's enough girls! Pour the tea for everyone. I'll take Aunty Bertha a cup. Then look for her cat and put it in its travelling basket. I'll find some clothes and things for her and we can all go home.'

Over tea, the attractive man introduced himself as John and before leaving told Nancy to let him know if there was anything he could do to help. What a day, she thought wearily and there'd be more difficult times ahead. Still, she smiled to herself, she wouldn't mind getting to know John. Would he be the silver lining to this particular cloud?

Eve

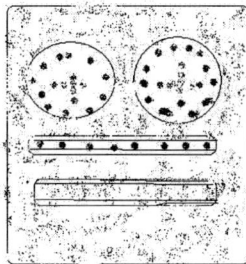

No More Fear

They had moved from refuge to refuge, but he had always found them.

It was not now for herself that she worried, but more for the other women and their children. Why should they have to be involved in the awfulness that had been her life?

It was time to stop running, and - what was it that Kirsty, from Women's Aid, was always chanting? - 'Feel the Fear and do it anyway.'

It's my fault really because I'm so clumsy, but I get nervous when Simon comes and stands behind me, watching. It's like he's waiting for me to make a mistake. But I don't always know what I'm doing wrong until it's too late. And then I drop things because I'm shaking, and anyway, it's better to get it over with because the waiting for it to happen is worse than when he actually does it. Sometimes the food's not hot enough or I've ironed his trousers with a crease down the front. I *know* he said that's how he wanted them ... but he keeps changing the rules and makes me muddled and I can never get it right.

Lately, Jamie's begun to annoy him. I tried to tell Simon that Jamie needs some small space to keep his toys, but he says I'm a useless slut and should keep things tidy.

Yesterday I had a phone call from Mrs Edwards from the Nursery School. Would I give her five minutes when I pick Jamie up tomorrow? She sounded cold and a bit cross, not like she is usually.

Mrs Edwards told me that Jamie had hit a little girl with a toy car and cut her head. She said the other mother was going to make a complaint but she wanted to talk to me first. Was everything all right at home? She said that Jamie got 'quite angry' sometimes, and hit the other children if they were playing with something he wanted. He was 'disruptive and aggressive.'

'But he's only a little boy,' I said, shocked.

'Yes,' she said, and repeated, 'Is everything all right at home?'

I couldn't tell her about the hitting could I? You can't have other people knowing your business. And I was upset about what she'd said about my lovely Jamie. He's not like that. He's the best thing I have in all the world. 'Specially since I lost my other one when I was six months gone. It was a little girl and I was going to call her Jade because that's a lovely colour. I'd told him to get off of me and that I didn't want sex as it would hurt the baby, but he had sex with me anyway and I fell asleep. I find that the only way to keep the peace is to have sex with him, which I don't want to do, but it does work sometimes.

I didn't tell the doctor how it happened and he said it was Mother Nature's Way of letting only the strongest of the species survive. I thought, Fuck Mother Nature.

When we got home, I asked Jamie about the car and hitting the little girl.

'But Daddy does it. And I wanted the car,' he said, looking down at his feet. 'It was red - and new,' he added.

It's true he doesn't have anything new. Simon resents anything I spend on Jamie, though it's little enough, heaven knows. All his toys have come from friends or jumble sales. I thought today that he has nothing that had not been worn or played with before. If I had my own money, I would buy him a new car, but Simon says I'm useless with money so he does all the buying. And he does work very hard to earn it for us. Then I cried.

The Guilty Suitcase

*

I must do something about myself. It's true what Simon says; I do look a mess. I'll start with my hair.

The picture on the packet of the smiling blond girl looks nothing like me. I must have got it wrong again. It's gone gingery, but only in streaks. I'll wear a scarf to school.

My sister says I'm so lucky to have Simon. 'He's an absolute charmer, Liz, much nicer than all the awful men I seem to meet. Hand him over when you're done,' she says, joking like, but she's not. 'Though you'll have to beat our Mother to the start.'

My friend Tamzin used to come round a lot to see me, but she and Simon never hit it off, and he used to be a bit rude to her. Simon told me later that she'd slagged me off to his sister who she knows through work. I thought she was my best mate.

'We don't need outsiders, my darling,' he'd say, 'we've got each other, all cosy in our little family, no need for others to come poking their noses in where they're not wanted.'

I love it when he calls me his darling. It makes me feel all warm and good inside, so I don't see Tamzin much now. She phones and asks if we can meet up for a drink one evening, but I wouldn't go behind Simon's back. I know he wouldn't like it. Haven't got any money anyway. So I never go.

Simon always hits me on my head. He told me the reason he hits me there is because no one can see the bumps and bruises. They never show up on photographs. When I called the Police the first time he said if I went to court, they wouldn't believe me, and they'd take Jamie away because it would show I was a bad mother and couldn't be trusted to look after him properly. I told the Police I wasn't going to press charges. The Police gave me a Crime Report number and said they'd *Look out for him.*

Then he hits Jamie.

He said he was sorry, couldn't think what came over him. There were problems at work - not his fault, but he was pretty stressed by it. It would all be different now. That, and how much he loved me.

Jamie won't go to sleep now without me giving him an extra cuddle and lots of goodnight kisses. Simon says I'm molly-coddling him. 'He'll turn into a poof, the way you go on,' he says. I think it's because he's jealous of the attention I'm giving Jamie and not him.

Then this, this very last time Simon got careless. I'd laid the knives and forks the wrong way round - always been left-handed and can't get out of the habit. 'Is it really too much to ask that you get this simple little thing right? Even *you* with *your* limited intelligence should be able to manage that!'

He hits me in front of Jamie now as if it doesn't matter. Jamie tried to get in between and pull him off and Simon shoved him away, but he landed against the corner of the table and his eye started to swell right up. Jamie started to cry and that really got Simon going. 'Now see what you've made me do,' he shouted, and picked up the kitchen scissors.

I never thought it would take this long to come to court. The Police have been great and so has Kirsty. I thought after they arrested him he'd go to prison straight away, but when I got out of hospital I found he was out on bail. The County Court did this paper which said he mustn't come near or contact me or Jamie but he's clever and finds out where we are. Funny thing is though, I'm not frightened of him any more. Once you've had the worst, you stop being frightened.

At court, the lady from the Witness Service explains what will happen. Their job is to look after witnesses and she says I can go into a small room and give my evidence on a video camera without having to face him in open court. I laugh and say that's exactly what I *do* want. I try to tell her about fear and getting over it and I think she understands.

He looks slight sitting there hunched up behind the glass wall in the dock. I look at him just the once and feel only surprise that this slightly overweight and balding man should have taken away so much of our lives. Surprise, and a small amount of pity.

'Can we go to Macdonald's, Mum?' Jamie asked afterwards.

'We can go anywhere we like, my love,' I said, knowing that at last it was true.

Eileen

Déjà Vu

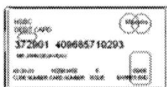

I had an idyllic childhood, not that I realised this during those nurturing years: the solid background, with a lovely home and grounds, staff to keep everything in order and running smoothly, dogs, ponies, holidays, outings round and about in Bristol. There always seemed to be guests visiting, which added to our lives, as we would involve the visitors both inside and outdoors whenever possible. Sometimes we would be allowed to stay up during the holidays or on other special occasions to listen to someone playing the piano or singing, even doing conjuring tricks, which captivated Alistair, my brother. My sister, Serena, loved the festivities and all that went with them, whereas I would wander off more often than not to find Queenie, the cook. She, whilst bustling away, would tell me stories about my father and grandparents for whom she had worked as a girl. Sometimes she would ask me to go and get some fruit and vegetables from her husband Jock, the gardener. They lived in a little cottage behind the house and we children felt quite at ease there. Alistair went off to boarding school and Serena and I followed a year later, but as the schools were nearby, we sometimes came home at weekends. Our friends came with us, which was great fun and we, in turn, visited them which was even more fun.

When I was fifteen we returned home for an exeat and straight away sensed that there was something wrong. Our parents asked us into the study and once seated, Daddy pronounced that there were going to be massive changes to our lives, which we would find very hard at first, but we must accept the changes and adapt. We were young and there would be many opportunities for us in the future. I remember we looked at each other, then at Mummy, who was sitting quietly, hands clasped together in her lap, tears streaming down her cheeks, then back to gaze at our father who seemed strangely subdued. Daddy took a deep breath and proceeded to tell us that the house was to be sold and that we would leave school at the end of term. Most of the furniture and our beloved ponies would have to go. Everything – everything would be lost. Jock and Queenie would be going to live with their son far away and so could not take the dogs – homes must be found for them. Our comfortable, carefree life came to an end that chilly October afternoon.

We went to live with our maternal Grandparents, who tried to give us a happy time at Christmas. In the past they had always come to our home, full of laughter and people, and so a quiet time was very sobering.

In the January we attended the local school and in time took up the threads of a new life. A few months after moving in with the grandparents, our parents went off to the Middle East to work for a British company and, by the following August, Alistair passed his A levels with good grades, which led to university and employment in the City. Serena won a scholarship to drama school but then went on holiday visiting our parents. Here she fell in love, which happily led to a wedding, followed quickly by three offspring. All too soon, Alistair met and married a charming girl, whilst I became increasingly conscious of feeling isolated in a quagmire of self-pity. I had one boring job after another, no particular friends, very little money, dreadful digs – nothing to aspire to. Every morning I felt sick in my stomach and wondered if I would ever climb out of my depression.

One evening, I decided to be positive and stop feeling sorry for myself and signed up the next day for a course in computer programming, having to borrow the money from Grandma. Then something happened – I can't explain, but it was as if a light came on! I completed the course with flying colours, applied for and got a junior position in a multi-national company. Things were looking up.

I moved to a new apartment in the centre of town, on my own this time. Having paid Grandma back, I began to enjoy life once more. Slowly, step by step: some new clothes, a holiday, outings to theatres, concerts and making a new circle of friends. Saving money at last, after paying my bills each month, I no longer felt ashamed and began to relax in my new environment. Then I met Christopher.

Christopher seemed to creep into my very being and it was as if he had always been part of me and my existence. Life was wonderful, nothing seemed to go wrong, I was swept off my feet. This man and his lifestyle were intoxicating. He was generous to a fault and he and his friends were self-assured, nothing seemed to faze them. Gradually I settled into a comfortable routine of dinner parties, holidays to exotic locations, weekends in the country, flights to Paris for lunch, weddings; it was nothing to fly to America or Australia for such an occasion.

It started in a small way, paying off things for Christopher as he had forgotten his credit card, lost his credit card, someone owed him a lot of money. Eventually he asked to see the jewellery my grandmother had given me. This was too much; the only thing I had from the past to give my future children. It was happening again. I was going to lose everything. I had given all my savings to the man I adored and believed in. I was in debt and afraid my job was at risk. What had I done? I felt history repeating itself. I would end up homeless, not belonging anywhere, getting old alone and becoming ill. How could I have been so stupid to be taken in? Only recently my father had told me that he had lost everything because he had lent a great deal of money to his brother and so caused our family terrible distress. I can't bear it. No! No! No!

'Abigail, Abigail, wake up! You're having a nightmare. That's what comes of falling asleep in the sun. What on earth were you dreaming about? Come, give me your hand. The children will be home from school soon and we must get ready for this evening.'

With the children safely tucked up in bed, David, my wonderful husband, and I leave them with the nanny and depart for the restaurant to meet his business associates for dinner.

After a long drawn out meal, I am relieved when the bill arrives so David can settle it and we can go home. My heart misses a beat when David, having discreetly checked his wallet, turns to me.

'Darling, I seem to have forgotten my credit card. Will you pay the bill?'

Elaine

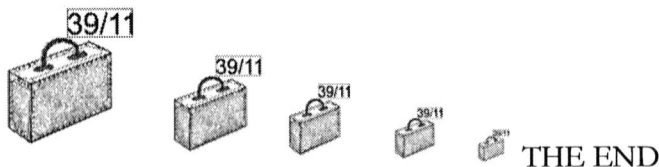

THE END